Kate Manton

Man's Wrongs

Woman's Foibles

Kate Manton

Man's Wrongs
Woman's Foibles

ISBN/EAN: 9783337396107

Printed in Europe, USA, Canada, Australia, Japan

Cover: Foto ©Andreas Hilbeck / pixelio.de

More available books at **www.hansebooks.com**

MAN'S WRONGS;

OR,

WOMAN'S FOIBLES.

BY

KATE MANTON.

BOSTON:
CROSBY & DAMRELL,
100 WASHINGTON STREET.
1870.

I.

IN the following pages I have given to *man*, the place which God has given him; — to *woman*, I present her foibles and vanities, that she may see herself as others see her; trusting that she will derive benefit from the sight.

The incidents of history, and those which have most deeply interested me in my travels, I trust will be of equal interest to all who may read them.

The entries of my love affair, I am free to confess, are tame and commonplace; but my retired life during the past year, has saved me from the stratagems and wiles which are requisite to a popular love story.

WANTED. "A partner with a capital of a thousand dollars in a business, the profits of which will be four thousand the first year."

A thousand dollars! Can I not devise some plan to earn it, secure the partnership and present it to my dear father?

Not that I care for wealth on my own account, for my wants are few, and my blessings far more than I deserve; but for my mother, — my kind, my gentle mother! When I think of her social position in by-gone days, her luxurious Southern home, her every wish anticipated, the greatest men of the day proud to be classed among her friends — and now, yes! and now, where is she?

Living on an obscure street in Harlem, a loved wife, and the almost idolized mother of her son and daughter; ever planning and contriving to meet the expenses of her family, on my father's scanty salary of fourteen hundred a year; denying herself, and us all, of every luxury, rather than owe any man a penny, and I, poor insignificant being that I am, earning just enough by my six drawing scholars to keep myself in plain clothes.

But then I am content.

Ma says "we should not try to deceive people by wearing finery and trinkets, giving them the impression that we are *not* poor when we *are* poor"! She says " when poverty is our misfortune rather than our crime, we should never be ashamed to say we cannot afford this, that, or the other, for such a course would win the respect of any man whose opinion was worth anything "; — and poverty *was* our misfortune, brought on by our wicked war!

Though we were loyal, and always have been loyal, *as* pa says, — for I neither know or care anything about politics, — to the best government on earth, yet our loyalty did not save us, for grandpa and pa were misrepresented by our countrymen, who were angry that they would not join with them in separating from the North; and thus, as brother Francis says, "help mar the glory of the grand old stars and stripes"! And so our slaves were taken, — I'm glad of *that*, if they are only treated well, for I never did believe in Slavery, — our elegant mansion was turned into barracks for the soldiers, our barns and grounds were destroyed, and we driven out to commence life anew in the cold, unsympathizing North.

How glad I am that uncle Frank insisted on investing that eight thousand of ma's in Bowditch's office, in Boston, — the " hub," as the Bostonians call it, — but *I* think they are very *pretentious*, when *New York* is so much more deserving the name!

Grandpa was a little touched about it at the time, — but had he have deposited it in one of our Southern offices, where would it have been now?

Echo answers, Where?

And now for the thousand dollars that I must try and earn; or if I could raise five hundred even, it may be by that time it would produce a partnership worth twenty-five hundred, or three thousand; for money is in such demand just now, that the inducements offered for its use are so fabulous, that one is inclined to doubt whether they are *bona fide* or no!

But this one reads as if it means what it affirms. If it should prove a humbug, the money that I earn will be no phantom, and in that case I can use it to assist in defraying brother Francis's expenses in Harvard.

I like old Harvard!

Grandpa and uncle Frank graduated there.

How I do love to hear them tell about their college days, particularly when they were Freshmen, and hazed! They never appeared to feel so sore about it as do the young collegians of the present day.

I always smile when I think of uncle Frank walking around his room with his nightcap on, drawing a little lamb on rollers, singing all the while, "Mary had a little lamb — little lamb — little lamb" — which feat was continued until he had made the circuit of the room thirty times! He says that " he never sees a lamb now, especially a *tin* one, that he doesn't smile."

And now, let me strike the anvils of my imagination, and see if a few sparks will emit, which, by lighting in the right direction, will enable me to reap the sum which I so ardently desire!

Perhaps, if I should try, I could write a book, — but what shall it be about?

The truth is, I never could write a composition even when I was in school, and contrived all sort of plans to procure a little help, and rid myself, in some way, of the hated duty.

Apropos. I cannot understand how the writing of compositions originated as a school exercise! Why not as well compose music or poetry, as prose?

The idea of *obliging* a child who has scarcely an idea in its little pate to write at least a page on " Benevolence," " Conscience," " Moral Suasion," and such like, with the knowledge that its poor attempt is to be paraded before the school, and, in some instances, the poor wight himself being called upon to read his own production. I do not believe the sin of deceiving,— yes! and lying often, will be laid at the door of those poor children who are actually *frightened* into wrong-doing.

Writing is a gift which few comparatively receive. There are those who could not write six pages, or even three, on a given subject, that could be called *writing*, to save their lives.

This exercise, I think, should be free,— without compulsion,— and children encouraged rather than driven to take up the study. I fear, though, as the talent and learning of the day are arrayed against me, it will be a long day before there will be reform according to my ideas!

But my book!

What shall be its title? for there's much in a name!

There was Mr. or Miss Hamilton,— it is difficult to tell whether *Gail* is masculine or feminine,— masculine, I should say, probably derived from Gaius, — who I doubt not has made twice the sum I desire, by the sale of the book, " Woman's Wrongs ; "

though I am free to confess a handsome portion of it should be sent to poor Dr. Todd, the free use of whose name, doubtless, contributing largely to the sale of the book.

Suppose I write on *Man's* Wrongs, — though it is precious little I know of man. I do not believe one-half that is said against him; at any rate, I should not be afraid to trust *my* happiness in the keeping of some one of the little dears! As far as I can judge, I think *man* has quite as many *wrongs* as woman; though if all were like my pa and ma, there would be no necessity for such a word in connection with human beings.

Should I speak my honest conviction, I should say that woman must thank *herself* for a great many of *her* wrongs, as she is pleased to call them. She prefers to read in her Bible the *duties of husbands*, that they should love and be tender of their wives, as their own bodies; omitting the weightier matters incumbent on herself, — as *reverence, subjection, submission!*

Grandpa says, " A kind wife makes a kind husband."

Grandpa is a judge, and he ought to know; though I remember when I went to school there were exceptions to rules, — but there is the door-bell, and I hear Minnie's voice!

II.

ON one of the principal avenues in Berkshire is an elegant mansion, surrounded by terraces and grounds in the highest state of cultivation. Arbors, fountains, and statuary abound; trees of every kind and size furnish a home for multitudes of songsters, who are constantly flitting from branch to branch, pouring from their tiny throats such a volume of melody as to impress the beholder with the belief that he must be on some Italian shore. Seated in one of these arbors is an elderly lady, discussing with her son the plans for his future career.

They are the widow and son of Sir Henry Stuart Vernon, formerly a wealthy barrister of Berkshire, who, at his decease a few weeks previous, had left his only son, then a student in Oxford, the present Sir Henry, an income of forty thousand a year, with the next claim to the title and fortune of his uncle,

Sir Albert Fortescue Vernon, Earl of Somerset. It had been the earnest wish of the elder Sir Henry that his only child should wed the fair Alice, eldest daughter of Lord Irving of Northumberland, one of the reigning belles, and heiress to one of the greatest fortunes in the county.

But young Henry, though a dutiful and obedient son in other respects, on this point was invulnerable, — positively declaring that he would never be tied for life to one whom he could neither love or respect.

"I have money enough of my own, so I surely shall not throw away my whole future happiness for money," said he.

"The Lady Alice Irving is haughty, cold, and self-opinionated. She never would yield her wishes to any one, especially a husband.

"No! if I am caught in the wiles of matrimony, it will be with some lady of character and heart; one who will feel for me so strong an affection, that a difference between us will be among the impossibilities.

"I care not for title or wealth!

"My wife, if I am ever blessed with one who is worthy the name of wife, will share my purse and title, and if I secure her heart in return, it is enough." So spake Sir Henry Vernon.

It was for the purpose of discussing this matter that his mother had requested an interview with him; all that *her* heart desired, was unbounded wealth and social distinction. For this, she had bartered herself to the elder Sir Henry, and *for* this she was willing to dispose of the future well-being of her only child.

" Love is a myth!" said she.

" There is no such thing to be found in this enlightened age. The present aim of every man and woman is, how they can best secure a connection with one who will add in some way to their own aggrandizement."

" Then, mother, how dare men enter the church, stand before the altar in the presence of God, and promise to love and cherish one in whom they have no delight?

" How can a woman stand before the same altar, and promise audibly, in the presence of the same great Being, to love, submit to, and reverence a man, for whom, alas! too often, she has not even a preference?

"Ah, mother, there is something wrong here! I would not perjure myself in this way to secure a throne; far sooner would I earn my bread by the sweat of my brow.

"The Lady Alice Irving I can never wed; I would rather be a lone wanderer on the earth, than pass a year with her, much less my whole life. She has my best wishes for her future happiness, but she will never be nearer to me than she now is, — an acquaintance only! I have no desire, even, to be entered on her list of friends!"

"My son," replied Lady Edith, "you are blind to your own interests. There was no love, — simply an every-day fancy, — between your father and me. We were both of us blessed with common sense! We knew very well that love will not pay for an establishment, or give social position; and as our union would place us both in a much higher standing than we could ever hope to attain if apart, we decided to marry, and entered into an alliance as we should any other business transaction; and you see we were *right*, my son!"

"This is a matter of opinion," replied Sir Henry, respectfully; "and I trust you will forgive me when

I say that the daily witness of the life which you and my father led, has been the great reason for my taking the decided stand which I now occupy."

" Do you mean to reflect on our treatment of each other?" inquired Lady Edith, haughtily.

" Did not your father and I ever maintain the utmost respect towards each other before the world?"

" Certainly, most certainly, mother; but God grant that I may never be so situated as to be obliged daily, nay hourly, to feign a respect which I do not feel! While my dear father lived, I ever tried to believe that I must be mistaken in my supposition, but your own words have proved my surmisings only too true. Again I say, God grant me strength to resist every temptation to connect myself with any one, if I cannot feel assured that love, — that perfect love of which the Bible speaks, — is to be the foundation of my union."

" Then, my son," replied Lady Edith, rising, and scarcely able to suppress her wrath, " *then*, my son, the day that dawns upon your marriage with one of ignoble blood, sees you a stranger to your mother evermore ; " and with these words she left the arbor.

Sir Henry gazed after her, and exclaimed, " Oh !

my mother, my mother, what might you not have been to your husband and child had you have based your marriage on true affection? My poor dear father, how have you wronged yourself, and how deeply have you been wronged! I could read your heart when you knew it not; I was a witness, during your last sickness, of that earnest longing for some one who would whisper to you words of sympathy and love; one, who instead of delegating the duty to a nurse, would have considered it the sweetest privilege to bathe your fevered brow, and place the cordial to your lips. You would not own it to me, my father, but I know that you were made for love; that when you were lying sick and low, you would have given all your wealth, if need be, to have received one loving word, one tender kiss — *kiss*, did I say? I don't believe you ever knew the meaning of the word in your own experience! and yet, — what am I saying? what am I thinking? It is my mother! I must draw a veil over her shortcomings, and not allow myself to dwell upon them, for I am commanded to *honor* my father and my mother. May God forgive me if I cannot do it!"

III.

A PARTY! Laura Jenkins to have a party, and I, of course, not invited.

I am not in society now.

And yet I, Kate Manton, in all my poverty, would feel it to be great condescension on my part to visit *her*, the daughter of a fish-dealer, who has nothing to boast of but the aristocracy of wealth!

I am the granddaughter of Judge Blake, — the highest, most respected, elegant gentleman of the old school, — and with *his* blood in my veins, that she should dare look down on me!

But stop! In what feelings am I indulging? Is this the charity that thinketh no evil? What can Laura Jenkins know of my antecedents? Just nothing! I am a drawing teacher with six pupils, the daughter of the "Clerk of the House," who has the paltry income of fourteen hundred a year on which to support a family of four, — house-rent, fuel, gas, food and clothing, all included. How soon we shall grow rich on this generous stipend! Laura Jenkins would spend twice the amount on herself alone, in the same length of time, and of course she looks down on me! But there is one consolation. All who are acquainted with our history feel that the condescension would be on our side. Give me superiority of intellect and culture, rather than that of wealth. In my case, however, I fear the one would prove quite as much of a phantom as the other!

But why should such a trifle annoy me? How much of real pleasure did I ever experience from the elegant parties which I attended before the dreadful war?

My own party, which pa gave for me on my entrée into society. Would not some of the young ladies who now look down upon me, be astonished at the elegance of that affair?

And yet, after all, when I compare those days with the present, I really think I lie down to sleep with a much happier heart now than I did then. It was ever a constant vying one with the other

which should excel in dress, in general appearance,
in dancing, in music; in a word, which should be
the observed of all observers! Should one more
happy than the rest chance to secure a little more
admiration and attention than the others, what heart-
burnings, what jealousies, what envyings! Still, I
must confess that it is rather hard for one who has
been educated in the highest school of refinement,
to be brought so low that even second-class people
will look down upon her!

But we are not separated entirely from our friends.
A few choice ones stand by us yet; but they are
those who stand on their own solid foundation, and
no one dare say to them, "Why do ye so?"

It is only those who stand on slippery places who
are afraid to extend the hand of fellowship to those
less blest in substance!   .

But I am ashamed of my weakness!

Had any one have told me that a trifling slight
like this should have thus aroused the evil in my
nature, I should have esteemed it an insult.

How much time I have wasted!

Had I have been patient under injury, I might
have written something on Man's Wrongs; but if

poor father waits for my inspiration, I fear it will be a long time before he sees brighter days.

How glad I am that I gave my seat in the horse-car to that poor woman this afternoon! Wasn't she grateful? Poor thing! I did pity her so.

How awkward to enter a car when every seat is taken, and find that you are standing alone, — the object of general surveillance to those who have been more fortunate than yourself. Your form, dress, and person scanned from top to toe. Some-times, if your garment is a trifle out of style, al-though it is the best you can afford, a smile, per-chance a whisper, will be exchanged, and significant glances thrown from one to the other, which will disconcert any modest young lady. Some young ladies assume an air of nonchalance, striving to show by their manner that they are not at all annoyed, they have a preference for standing; but any one of ordinary discernment can see at a glance that it is only a disguise of momentary irritation!

Didn't those young ladies who sneered at me for offering my seat to the poor woman, look unutter-able things when that elegant stranger rose and proffered me his seat?

I suppose some fault-finders would ask why he did not rise for the poor woman? He was at the extreme end of the car, and did not see her till she was in the act of taking my seat. I declined accepting it as long as propriety would admit, for I cannot accept the seat of another, as many people do, as a right! Such a look of admiration as he gave me, when I politely thanked him. It more than compensated me for performing what I conceived to be my duty. And here it will not be inappropriate for me to write a word on what I consider one of "Man's Wrongs."

Why every man who wishes to be considered a gentleman, should feel obliged, no matter how weary he may feel, to rise and proffer his seat whenever a lady enters a car, I cannot comprehend.

I am sorry to say if this is the criterion of a gentleman though, the laboring classes would be in the majority.

Ma says it was etiquette in her day for no gentleman to sit in the presence of a lady while she remained standing. It was a mark of respect for the lady; but, in our day, there are those who think the less respect they show for the presence of ladies, the more independent will they be considered.

I have heard, on good authority, that there are men in Boston, calling themselves gentlemen, who will rush for the horse-car the moment it arrives at the starting-point, and will so push and jostle one another that they may secure a seat for themselves, it is dangerous, at times, for a lady to attempt entering until these same *gentle*men(?) have monopolized every seat. This does not sound well, and is not at all for the credit of our sister city.

But this evil can be remedied. The trouble is, too much is expected of man in this particular. He has *his* rights, and they should be respected. He should never be asked, by a *look* even, to give up his seat. Should he be kind enough to waive his right for the accommodation of a fellow-passenger, let him be cordially thanked for his politeness.

The selfishness, the coarseness, the want of true modesty in so many of the women of the present day; the accepting every favor as though it were a right, has done much to cause men, in many respects, to act so contrary to their better nature.

Before so much was said of *woman's* rights, man

considered himself as her protector ; but as the world progresses, and he finds that she prefers to take care of *her*self, — he, acting on the same principle, concludes to look our for *him*self !

I do not blame him.

Man has his rights, and he intends to maintain them.

One may always recognize, however, a gentleman of the *old* school !

He cannot yet bring himself to sit while a lady remains standing; and others who have been educated in this belief, will not be convinced that any one *is* a gentleman who does not, at least, proffer his seat, although he may not insist on its being accepted.

JANUARY 6th.

To-day is mending-day. It is a mystery to me how ma can contrive to do all her mending in one day, when we have so few clothes, and are obliged to wear them till it appears as if a touch even would tear them. She acts upon the principle, "A stitch in time saves nine ! "

As we sewed, we discussed Laura Jenkins's party. Ma thinks my views and feelings are very wrong.

She says "America is very different from Europe," which, of course, I knew before.

She says "there is no such thing as nobility of descent in America; that men in this country depend mainly on their own efforts for position in society. Should the richest, most refined, and cultivated people, occupying the highest social position, trace back their genealogy for one or two generations only, they will find that their grandparents, and in some cases their parents even, lived in two or three rooms, were coopers, bricklayers, shoemakers, or mechanics of some sort, who, by their industry and unostentation, laid by a small sum, which, by accumulating, enabled them to educate their children, and give them advantages of which they themselves were deprived, and at their death to leave them a handsome fortune. This, combined with education, sound sense, and observation, has given to them an ease and grace of manner which ever elicits the admiration of the world."

Ma says "it is of no use for one to put on airs in these days, and feel above another whose father, perchance, is a country grocer! She must be very careful that she herself does not live in a glass house, and learn, to her chagrin, that her own grandfather was a country tailor!

She says, also, that " it is the mark of a very weak mind to be constantly on the alert to ascertain a person's pedigree before you dare have any intercourse with them. Those who are called *shoddy*, to-day, will be the merchant princes in a few more years, and an acquaintance will then be desirable with their children, as much as it is now deprecated. In our land it is the law of rotation; — 'One goes up, and the other goes down!'"

IV.

MINNIE MAVERICK has been in this afternoon, and has told me all about the party.
She said "she did not care particularly about going,
although Laura was a very amiable and accomplished young lady; but as her father desired her
to accept, she did so on his account."

I overheard pa saying to ma that "Maverick was
working for an election to Congress next year, so
that it was policy for him to ingratiate himself into
the good graces of all."

Minnie Maverick lives on Fifth Avenue. Mr.
Maverick is one of Wall Street's wealthy brokers,
and I trust I am not uncharitable when I say that
"I think the reason he permits Minnie to be so intimate with me, is the fact that father was a prominent lawyer in Milledgeville, and that Judge Blake
is my grandfather." Though fate obliges us to live

in obscurity for a time, yet the day may dawn when we shall be enabled to take our former position.

Minnie says "she was completely taken by surprise. She had supposed the party to be a small, every-day affair, so she dressed herself accordingly, and ordered her carriage to convey her there just after eight, and to call her at half-past ten.

"What was her chagrin, on arriving, to find that she was the first of the invited guests; and, to add to her discomfiture, she saw at once that the preparations were on such a scale, it was to be a large and elegant party, and it would be an hour, at the least, before the other guests would arrive." But Minnie is well educated, self-possessed, and equal to any emergency. Although not elegantly, yet she was becomingly dressed. She therefore told Laura, without hesitation, that "she had been laboring under a mistaken impression in regard to the party, and that she would doubtless appreciate the awkwardness of her position."

Laura appeared with such quiet dignity, and yet entered into her feelings with such ready sympathy, that Minnie's heart has been completely taken by storm.

As Laura was obliged to absent herself for a short time, her father, Mr. Jenkins, exerted himself to play the agreeable, and thus cause Minnie to forget her annoyance.

Poor Minnie is as completely captivated by the father as the daughter.

"A fish-dealer!" she says. "If every one in her own circle, even if it is the 'elite,' was as perfect a gentleman as Mr. Jenkins, she shouldn't blame old Mrs. Rogers for calling them 'top-knots'!" "If I have any penetration," said Minnie, "I should think there were very few as high-bred as Mr. Jenkins. Nothing of affectation about him, but a quiet, self-possessed, and cultivated gentleman."

"Oh, Kate!" said Minnie, "you never saw a collection of such elegant paintings as they have at Laura's. I really feel that ours, of which I was always so proud, are scarcely worthy of being mentioned, even. It seemed to afford Mr. Jenkins real pleasure to point out their beauties, and give me their history. Two of them he purchased when in Spain. He was very fortunate in obtaining them, which he did through the influence of one of his wife's relatives whom they were visiting, as she was a personal friend of the original owner, and evinced much interest in procuring it for them. Laura's mother is of Spanish descent.

"One of the paintings was by Cano, surnamed El Racionero, who was born in Granada about the year 1600, and who was so distinguished that his countrymen called him the Michael Angelo of Spain. He was court-painter to Philip the Fourth. 'He had an ungovernable temper, and at one time was put upon the rack, on suspicion of having killed his wife in a fit of jealousy; but he was absolved from the charge. His right arm, however, was exempted from the torture, on account of his excellence in his art. Mr. Jenkins said, also, that 'he refused, when dying, to take the crucifix from the priest, on account of its bad workmanship.'

"The other painting was by Murillo, who was born in Seville about eighteen years after Cano, and who died there about 1682. A short time before his death, he went to Cadiz to paint the espousals of St. Catharine, over the altar in the Capuchin church in that city; and while engaged on the work, he fell from the scaffolding, and the wound proved fatal. He was buried in the church of Santa

Cruz, in Seville, before a picture of the 'Descent from the Cross,' by Campana, which he had greatly admired in his life.

"There was an exquisite Madonna of Raphael's, a painting of Vouet, — a celebrated French artist, — beside many smaller works of some of the masters. These hung in the drawing-room.

"The library adjoining was hung with pictures by other artists, among which were paintings by Copley, Turner, Fielding, and others of renown; and last, though not least, one of Bierstadt's elegant pictures.

"Beside the paintings, there were curiosities of every description; but before I had time to examine one-half of them, Laura returned. She was dressed in the sweetest dress of white muslin, without a jewel about her; a few exquisite camelias only in her hair, and a tea-rose in place of a brooch!

"The rooms were filled with the fragrance of flowers, which were scattered around in the greatest profusion.

"Laura's mother soon followed her, and is really an elegant woman. She has a dark, rich, olive complexion, with the blackest eyes and hair. She wore a dress of black satin, tastily trimmed with lace, and

the longest train I have seen this season. She is so
tall and noble looking, that altogether she was my
beau ideal of elegance, in every sense of the word.

"Shortly after, the other guests began to arrive.
Many of them I knew by name, but a few only
whom I had ever met before. They appeared, however, quite as much at ease as they do in our own
circles; and, between us, Kate," said Minnie, "I
think there is a great deal of humbug about our
being the elite! To be sure there are some among
us who act as if they really believe they are made
of better flesh and blood than men at large, but
I am beginning to be enlightened in this respect."

"What of the supper?" asked I.

"The table looked superbly," replied Minnie.
"Solid silver, cut glass, and the most exquisite china
adorned it, interspersed with the most fragrant and
magnificent pyramids of flowers that I have ever
seen. There was the greatest profusion of niceties
and delicacies, of every name and kind, the whole
under the direction of six black waiters who were
in attendance.

"I forgot to tell you, Kate," said Minnie, "that

I was introduced to Laura's brother, who arrived
from Europe last week.

"He is just through with his studies, — you know
he was in Oxford. He had with him the most distinguished looking stranger I ever saw, and whom
he introduced as Mr. Vernon.

"Laura told me afterward that he had lately lost
his mother, and that he was to travel from six
months to a year in America. Also that he was
engaged to a young English lady by the name of
Irving. They say it is not a love-match, but he
engaged himself to her to please his mother, who
was very anxious they should be united.

"One thing I must confess, to my shame! Minnie mentioned me casually while talking with Laura,
who said she had never heard of me. She regretted
it exceedingly, as it would have afforded her much
pleasure to have included me among her guests.
Minnie was kind enough to say that 'although the
invitation would have afforded *me* much pleasure,
it was doubtful if I had accepted it, as my life
was *so* changed, and I went out but very little. I
had been suddenly transplanted from a luxurious
Southern home, to a home in what I dignified 'the

cold, unsympathizing North!' I suppose the North-erners will resent my unwarrantable assertion, as they will deem it; but I only affirm what I really believe to be true, when I say, 'there is as much differ-ence in the characters and habits of the inhabitants of our Southern States from those of the Northern portion, as in their climate.'

"To-morrow I am to take tea socially with Minnie. I do enjoy it so much, — I am so strongly reminded of my own Southern home; the attentive colored waiter anticipating, at the right moment, your every wish. Forgive me, if I *do* sigh for the good old days of yore; and yet I believe that patience is having its perfect work, and that in patience I shall yet possess my soul!"

3

V.

TRUTH *is* stranger than fiction!

To think that I should meet again my hero of the horse-car!

Yesterday, about four o'clock, Minnie called for me in her barouche, and we took a delightful drive through Greenwood Cemetery.

There is something peculiarly solemn, and yet intensely interesting, to me, in visiting a cemetery, especially where everything bears such unmistakable evidence of care and affection for the loved dust. It is one of my favorite haunts, —

"Far from the abode of man and strife."

As we drove through the rustic gateway, and beheld the long aisles of this great temple, with its dark branches meeting overhead, in arches much more graceful than any formed by the hand of man, while here and there rose the monuments erected to the departed, I thought I had never seen a fitter receptacle for the ashes of those who have gone before. The wind whistled mournfully among the trees, and the waters, as they washed the shore, sent forth a melancholy dirge, but it was in keeping with my feelings.

One of the first spots that we visited was Indian Mound, on which is a monument bearing a sculptured figure of a mourning Indian warrior. It was erected to the memory of Do-Hum-Mee. She was a Sachem's daughter of the Sac Indians, who visited Washington with her father, and who was married before arriving at New York, to a young Iowa chief, who was of their party. Shortly after her marriage she took a violent cold, which resulted in her death while yet in New York, and before she had been married many days. She was only eighteen years of age, and her death occasioned a profound sensation.

In Locust Avenue, near Southwood, we were attracted by a singular-looking monument, bearing the names of two ladies by the name of Cairns; one, one hundred and seventeen years old, the other, one hundred years. Minnie says that "for a long time there were glass jars affixed to the gate and fence-posts, which contained a fluid labelled 'Eden's Oil,' but they were supposed to have been stolen."

On Battle Avenue I saw a monument which reminded me of dear brother Francis, as it was to the memory of a school-boy, — " Our Fred " ! What feelings of gratitude welled in my heart, that it was not our Frank! How seldom we care or think even of the sorrows of others! My thoughts wandered back to the time when " Our Fred " was as full of buoyancy and hope as Francis now is, — and yet he had to lie down and die, leaving all the loved ones behind. Ah! it is not the old who alone are taken, and nothing will so impress one with the vanity of all things here below, as a visit to a grave-yard. This monument was a well-executed figure of a school-boy.

Near this was the imitation of a tree-trunk in white marble, leaning against which was a cross, — the whole overspread with sculptured vines and flowers.

As we passed along Highland Avenue, at the base of Chestnut Hill, we thought of the monument to Miss Canda, and turned towards Greenbough Avenue to look upon it.

Miss Canda was of French descent, who, returning from a party one evening, was thrown from her carriage and instantly killed. On Battle Avenue, at its junction with Greenbough, is a very magnificent monument of white marble, in the form of a Gothic Chapel, in a niche of which is a statue, which was meant as a likeness of Miss Canda. Flowers of different kinds hang in great profusion from the mouldings of the arches.

The initials " C. C.," upon a shield, is formed of seventeen rosebuds. On each of sixteen gablets is a bunch of flowers, and each bunch has seventeen roses. There is an oblong space in front of the statue, which is surrounded by a balustrade, forming a sort of porch to the monument. A monumental slab is in the middle of the space, having at its head an urn, with books and instruments of music and drawing scattered around; while upon the rose and jessamine branches which adorn the balustrade are little birds, of which the departed young lady was very fond. Numerous butterflies are scattered around, —emblems of the body released from the grave and ascending to the skies.

Leaving this sad but elegant offering to the departed, we passed on through Alder Avenue, Forest, and Woodland Avenues, to Woodland Ridge, to look upon the grave of Lieutenant Stone, who was killed at the battle of Gettysburgh. Minnie says he was only twenty years old, and that he was universally beloved.

We were anxious to mount the summit of Ocean Hill, but time would not allow. Minnie says "from its summit you can see the villages of Flatbush and New Utrecht; also Coney Island, with the blue sea skirting its curving shores." I wish I could pass a day, rather than two hours, visiting this beautiful spot, for I have but just begun to see its beauties; but Minnie assures me I shall drive out again with her before many days have elapsed.

I feel better for this visit to Greenwood. I feel more keenly than ever that this life is but the preparation for another, and that I shall yet find reason to praise God for the path through which He is leading me, though it is mostly dark and dreary, and I fear often I shall faint by the way.

As we were returning from our drive I saw two gentlemen approaching, who, as they drew near, raised their hats to Minnie with the most inimitable grace! Before I could recover from my surprise, Minnie ejaculated, "Isn't he splendid-looking?"

"Who? which?" said I. "Why, Minnie, one of them is the identical gentleman who gave me his seat in the horse-car! Where *have* you seen him? Who is he? tell me quick, for I am almost beside myself with curiosity."

"First, Katy dear, you must inform me why you are so agitated! This is the first intimation that I have ever received, the quiet, dignified Miss Manton was interested in any one!

"Tell me his name, Minnie," I replied, "and I will tell you all you wish concerning the matter."

"The one nearest the barouche," replied Minnie, "was Laura Jenkins's brother; and the other, — your hero, — was Sir Henry Stuart Vernon, the wealthy barrister from England, who is engaged to an heiress, the Lady Alice Irving, of noble descent, and whom I told you I met at Laura's party. So, Katy dear,

we'll 'hang our harps on the willow-tree,' as far as
he is concerned!"

Ah! how little Minnie knew how my poor heart
went down, down, till I felt almost miserable.

I then told Minnie the incident as I confided it
to you, dear Diary! How was I startled to hear
her reply!

"Why, Kate Manton! Have you lived in New
York a year, and not yet discovered that it is a very
rare occurrence for a gentleman or lady to ride in
a horse-car? They patronize the omnibus almost
entirely, and the gentlemen are noted for their great
politeness to all who use this mode of conveyance.
How Sir Henry came in a horse-car is the first
mystery, and how you came there yourself is the
second!"

"For Sir Henry, I cannot answer; but for myself,"
replied I, "I am so exhausted after giving my
drawing-lessons, I am very glad to go home in the
way which requires the least effort, and I must admit
I vastly prefer the horse-car. They are patronized
by people of the highest respectability in other
places."

"Very true," replied Minnie, "and are used here,

if necessity require. There is no disgrace in riding in them during the day, but they are very undesirable in the evening."

"Why, Kate! what *is* the matter? You surely cannot have lost your heart, for you have not had so much as an introduction to Sir Henry."

I did not answer, although I felt that it was not at all necessary to be introduced to a gentleman before you can fall in love with him!

"For my own part," continued Minnie, "I am much more inclined to be fascinated with Arthur Jenkins. I think he is *superb!*"

"Yes! and after you are married you can have a carriage with the insignia of a fish!"

"Kate Manton," said Minnie, "how *bitter* you are! What *is* the matter with you?"

This speech recalled my wandering thoughts. I assumed an air of easy nonchalance; bantered Minnie about Arthur, and laughed to scorn the idea of my — poor, insignificant, crest-fallen girl that I am — of my lifting my thoughts for a moment to Sir Henry Stuart Vernon. Miserable deception! My heart was sick, though, and I could not prevent it.

No one but myself knew, and no one else should

ever know, how that one admiring, sympathizing glance which he bestowed on me in the car, sank into my soul. How eagerly I tried to extract comfort from the thought that even if he was engaged, it was only to please his mother!

Soon after our arrival home, tea was announced; and, as soon as we had supped, we hastened to Minnie's room, to prink a little, in case we should be favored with calls in the evening.

Minnie declared "she had a presentiment that the two strangers would call."

I insisted upon it that she should give me some reason for so thinking; but she positively declared "that nothing, save an indescribable secret feeling, occasioned the remark."

"They will *not* see *me*, if they do call," replied I, "for they will have to become acquainted with my present position!"

"You are a perfect mystery to me, Kate," said Minnie.

"Suppose you *are* in depressed circumstances, you are a lady! I have heard my father say, again and again, that wealth is no criterion in the mind of a true gentleman. He who would barter himself for wealth is *not* a gentleman. There could be no greater insult than for a man to win the affection of a woman, simply that he may aggrandize himself. I don't believe it possible for a genuine gentleman to be *selfish!*

"No, Kate; in this respect I think man is oft-times wronged. Man is of a nobler, stronger nature than woman. He is free from her foibles, her weakness. He feels that he *is* a man! He stands on his own foundation. He cares not for Mrs. D or Mrs. L's opinion; he acts according to the dictates of his own better judgment. A true gentleman cannot be a *snob.* Whenever I meet one of these deluded mortals, I always think I should like to shut him up in a farm-yard with a dozen peacocks, and oblige him to parade himself every day to the admiring crowd, till he came to his senses.

"I think if God has been pleased to bless one man with more of this world's goods than He has another, it is the very best reason why he can *afford* to be generous; and he *will* be so, if left to himself, — if no woman insinuates that he should not extend the hand of fellowship with Mr. G, simply because he counts his dollars by hundreds rather than thousands."

" Speaking of gentlemen, Minnie," said I, " reminds me of grandpa. Notwithstanding he is so highly educated, and of such high social position, he always takes the greatest pains to notice the poor, if they are educated and of modest demeanor.

" Of course he keeps aloof from those persons whose converse and bearing betoken vulgarity. There is so great a want of congeniality with such, that he cannot be blamed. If, however, he is thrown in the path of this class, he treats them with such marked politeness as ever to elicit the remark, ' He is every inch a gentleman ! '

" Now between us, Minnie, I think all this would sound very well on paper; but when it comes to the actual demonstration of such feeling, I plead guilty !

" I cannot help feeling that I am a little better than some who live on Fifth Avenue, even though they may be possessed of ten times our wealth. I know it is preposterous, but still there is the old latent pride in my heart.

" I struggle against it day by day, and am no

nearer rising above it than when I commenced the attempt; and yet, if I know my own heart, it is my very humiliated position that rouses such feelings; perhaps you will say, that reveals my true self.

"I believe if I should ever again be placed in my former position, I should *delight* to 'condescend to men of low estate!'"

"Well, Kate, it appears that we are sadly wandering from our mark, and not enlightening each other much on what constitutes a gentleman! To return from our starting-point: you do not wish to meet a gentleman simply because he is rich and you are poor. I think it is an absurd idea. Any man whose acquaintance is worth cultivating, will esteem you for yourself. You think that if Sir Henry should discover that you are poor, he will not care about placing you on his list of friends, and that if he has a penchant for you, the discovery of your poverty would turn the current of his feelings at once. I don't agree with you!

"I believe, Kate, in love. I do not believe in its being bought or sold. There are scores of marriages, day after day, without a particle of love between the parties; but may I be delivered from *such* a marriage!

"If I ever marry, the man that I wed must love me for myself alone. He must be as happy to wed me if a pauper, as though I were an heiress. Then, should we meet with reverses, which you know at this time are an every-day occurrence, we shall still be happy in one another. No sacrifice would be too great for me to make for the one I love, if I am assured that my love meets an equal return."

"Yes, Minnie," said I, " this is all true, and meets my views entirely; but how are you going to ascertain that you are loved for yourself alone? Your father is a millionaire, and you have the advantage not only of wealth, but beauty and grace combined. Of course Miss Minnie Maverick is one of the belles, and as such can bring almost any one she may desire to her feet."

"She has no desire for the worship of the many, Katy dear," replied Minnie.

"That is true," said I; "no one will ever accuse *you* of being a flirt, Minnie, any more than myself. *Simply a flirtation!* does not heal the wounded heart. Love, in my estimation, is a matter of too much moment for trifling."

"Candidly, Kate," said Minnie, "I have never, among all my many acquaintances, met with but one gentleman whom I think I could intrust with the keeping of my happiness!"

"Nor I either," replied I, quickly.

"Ah, Kate, be careful, my dear friend, and don't give your heart to one that can never be anything to you but a friend. I wish so much it could be. I warn you only because I love you so well, and I could not bear to see you miserable."

"I shall not be miserable, Minnie. My lot in life will be one of single blessedness. In fact I have never seen but the one being that I could possibly fancy; and I have common sense, so do not be uneasy about me, Minnie dear.

"Now there are pa and ma! No one could doubt for a moment but theirs was a marriage of true love. The wealth was on ma's side. Pa was rich in everything but gold, but no one could say he married ma for her lands! It was pure, perfect love between them, as time has fully proved.

"Think, Minnie, what a change for ma,—reared

in affluence, and now being obliged to turn over a
five-cent postal two or three times before she can
decide to spend it; and yet no sacrifice is too great
for her to make for pa, if she can only conduce to
his comfort. She does everything in such a quiet,
unostentatious manner, anxious only that he should
not discover the sacrifice!

"It does seem as though some women perfectly
admire to make a heroine of themselves in their
husbands' eyes! See what a sacrifice I am making
for you! See how hard I work to give you a neat,
comfortable home! Such a meek look of quiet
forbearance.

"For my own part, I should rather make an
open parade of it at once, and say to my husband,
'I've sacrificed *so* much, I have worked *so* long,
and *so* hard, just for you; and now what have you
got to say for yourself by way of thanks?'

"I should like to ask such wives what their husbands are doing in the way of work and sacrifice
for them?

"Not one wife in twenty knows the mental care
and anxiety with which almost every husband and
father returns to his own fireside at night. These

cares he leaves at the outer door, so that he may not add a single drawback to the happiness of his ittle family. I must say that I do not wonder the Bible makes man the *nobler* being, for I think, if you take him as a whole, he is, and I am willing to admit it.

"As to pa and ma, I never knew them to have a difference but once, and that was last voting-day.

"You know ma was born in Milledgeville; but pa was born in Lenox, Massachusetts, and always lived North till after he graduated; then he came to Milledgeville to practise law, and there he fell in love with my darling ma! Of course they were both strong Union in their politics, but ma was rather more conservative than pa. She favored Seymour's being President. She was ever talking about his being such a noble specimen of a Christian man; and though pa did not perfectly agree with her, yet he never contradicted her, or made any remark to irritate her.

"When the morning of voting-day arrived, uncle Francis looked in while we were at breakfast, and asked pa to be at the polls in good season, adding, '*Of course you'll vote for the General.*' Pa made no reply; but, with a look of recognition, went on eating his breakfast.

"As soon as uncle Frank closed the door, ma said, in a very excited manner, 'Charles Manton, if you vote for Ulysses Grant, there'll be *war* in the house! I had much rather you would not vote at all, than throw away your vote in this manner.'

"Pa waited a moment before speaking, and then said, 'Mary, do you think your husband competent to judge and act for himself, or do you wish to take his place? Be careful, dear, and don't let the first word of bitterness that ever came between us be on account of *politics.*'

"'Charles,' she soberly replied, 'I *do* love you, and I believe in your good sense and judgment; but if you only *could* vote for the noble Seymour, I should be *so* happy! I never *did* believe in a military man for a statesman! I suppose I must endure it, however. Oh, Charles, if women only *could* have their rights!'

"'Yes, darling, and you shall have yours this moment;' and with these words he caught ma, and giving her a good kiss on each cheek, said, '*These are woman's rights,* and they are all she ought to desire!'

"Ma laughed, and said that was one way to get over a wrong, and as long as pa was so true to her, she would try and be contented to let him adopt his own views as to being true to his country."

"Well," said Minnie, "my father is down on 'Womans' Rights.' He says that when the day arrives for women to go to the polls, there will be no such thing as *a home* for a man. He says Satan is trying to deceive the poor women, and make them feel that they are humiliated and wronged because they cannot cast their vote; but if the day shall ever arrive when their object is attained, he will then show the cloven foot, and there will be nothing but families at variance among themselves!"

Dear me! there's the dinner-bell, and I haven't written half that I wish; and as I must attend to my drawing-scholars this afternoon, I must wait till this evening to finish my account of my visit to Minnie's.

VI.

AND now, before I am interrupted, let me finish the account of my visit to Minnie's.

As soon as we had beautified ourselves, — we did powder just one little bit, though I must confess I feel a little cheap when I think of it, — we returned to the parlor. Just imagine a young lady receiving her first kiss, and finding the powder had gone from her forehead and remained on the gentleman's lips!

They say that the forehead is the place for the first stolen kiss; although as I have yet had no experience in such matters, I cannot answer for the truth of it! I'm sure, in such a case, I shouldn't blame the gentleman if it was not only the first, but the last kiss also!

Grandpa says "all who use powder are deluded! Their charms may be heightened, but once powdering is always powdering, and that, after its use for a time, the complexion without it is dreadful; and then, if man finds that the charms which attracted him are false, he will be very apt to turn away from the deceiver in disgust."

Well! this is my first time, and I mean it shall be the last, though I may not be so fair to look upon.

My weakness was that I wanted to look radiant in the eyes of Sir Henry Vernon, in case Minnie's presentiment should prove true. Weakness, indeed! wickedness, I should say, that I should desire for a moment to turn him from his allegiance to the Lady Alice Irving. How supremely ridiculous for me to allow myself to think of him for a moment! Sir Henry Vernon is as far from *my* reach, as the North from the South Pole.

We had scarcely reëntered the parlor when the door-bell rang.

"*Presentiment!*" said Minnie, while the fun danced in her eyes.

The door was thrown open, and the footman announced Sir Henry Vernon and Mr. Jenkins. After the usual form and ceremonies of introduction had passed, and the ordinary topics of the day had been discussed, Sir Henry asked Minnie if she sang.

"I do not," replied Minnie; "playing only is my forte. My friend Miss Manton sings."

"Why, Minnie! how can you?" said I.

"Will you not favor us, Miss Manton?" said Sir Henry.

Remembering my father's advice, that when a young lady was asked to play or sing it was not that she was expected to astonish her friends, but simply to gratify them as far as she was able, and how much more she would raise herself in the estimation of all by simply expressing her willingness to thus gratify them, rather than to waste, as some young ladies are in the habit of doing, many minutes with sundry excuses, and yet meaning at the same time to display their powers in the end. — ("This," he said, "was simply vanity, — that it took away one-half the charm of the music, and made the hearer much more inclined to criticise the performance. Not that he approved of flying to the piano the moment one was invited to play, and then monopolizing it to the exclusion of all other musicians, as it is the wont of some to do, but that there is a happy medium between the two that a sensible person will discover, and know how to conduct under all circumstances,") I replied to Sir Henry that " I sang a few simple ballads to gratify my own immediate friends, but as my style was simple, and I may say uncultivated, it would not be likely to please in general."

" There are times when simplicity of performance is more gratifying, and in accordance with the feelings of the listener, even if his taste is highly cultivated, than a more elaborate style;" and with these words he rose, and coming towards me, remarked, —

" I feel you will gratify us, Miss Manton ! "

Of course I could not refuse, and, accepting his proffered arm, he conducted me to the piano.

After playing a short prelude, I sang " Highland Mary," — one of Burns's sweet little songs. Sir Henry said that " it was very interesting to remember the circumstances under which it was composed. ' Highland Mary ' was Mary Campbell, who was the daughter of a mariner residing in Greenock. She became acquainted with Burns while on service at the Castle of Montgomery, where they plighted their mutual faith by the exchange of Bibles." He

said "that they stood with a running stream between them, and, lifting up the water in their hands,
vowed love while woods grew and waters ran. The
Bible which the poet gave was elegantly bound.
'Ye shall not swear by my name falsely,' was
written in it by Burns, and underneath the verse his
own name, and mark as a Freemason. Mary Campbell died, however, of a fever, and they parted to
meet no more."

Sir Henry said, also, "that he had seen the identical Bible, which was in the keeping of her relations, and also a lock of her hair." He said, also,
that "he scarcely knew which piece he preferred;
the 'Highland Mary,' or the 'Ode to Mary in
Heaven,' commencing, —

'Thou ling'ring star, with less'ning ray.'

This last was written on the anniversary of 'Highland Mary's' death."

I then sang the sweet little piece, —

"Oh Mary, go and call the cattle home!"

which elicited much admiration.

"Vernon," said Mr. Jenkins, "will you and Miss

Manton sing, for my especial benefit, the duet, 'See the pale moon'? I think it a perfect little gem."

After a moment's hesitation, Sir Henry replied, "I am out of practice entirely; still, if Miss Manton will permit me to accompany her, I shall be very happy to make the attempt."

While we were searching for the notes he said, in a low tone, "Miss Manton, have I not had the pleasure of meeting you before?"

I hesitated.

"In the horse-car?" he asked.

I nodded assent. He said nothing more, but such a look of admiration and respect as he gave me I shall never forget; and yet it isn't ten minutes since I declared that I would never think of him again, but would banish his image every time it came unbidden to my mind; but I *must* think of him a moment, just while I write these events in my Diary.

After we sang the duet I arose, and, leaving the piano, Sir Henry conducted me to my seat, and, taking a chair near me, we prepared to listen to Minnie, who had just consented to favor Mr. Jenkins with a suite, in C sharp minor, of William Sterndale Bennett's.

Sir Henry said that " he was proud to acknowl-
edge Bennett as an Englishman, although he must
admit that he owed a great deal of the beauty and
grace of his style to his great intimacy with Mendelssohn, with whom he was very intimate, and at
whose invitation he visited Leipsic, where he brought
out some of his works, which were received with
such favor that he was induced to make Germany
his home for many years."

Minnie also played, in a very sprightly manner,
a scherzo by Chopin.

I delight in the wild, soul-stirring harmonies of
Chopin!   One imagines himself in Poland, when
listening to the weird strains.·

That Chopin was a genius, rare and gifted, no one
will pretend to deny.   One cannot weary of listening to his varied productions, for even his waltzes
and impromptus, simple though they be, pour forth
a flood of melody.   Although there is such a wide
difference in the style of these two composers, yet
both are irresistible!

After the music had ceased, and a few moments
of general conversation had ensued, the gentlemen,
assuring us how much our music had contributed to

the pleasure of their call, and expressing the hope that they should soon meet us again, bade us good-evening, and withdrew.

For a minute Minnie looked at me, and I looked at Minnie.

"What do you think of presentiments, Kate?" said she.

"That they come true sometimes," said I, "though not always."

"Isn't Jenkins magnificent?" said Minnie.

"He is certainly very fine-looking," said I.

"Why don't you own up, Kate, and say not half so good-looking as Vernon?"

"Because I do not wish to," I replied.

"Why, Kate Manton! I do believe you've lost your heart," said Minnie.

"I have not the slightest doubt you have lost yours to Jenkins," I replied, "or you would not think of mentioning him in the same breath with Sir Henry. You know love is blind! But, Minnie, if you love me, do not quiz me about Mr. Vernon; for if you do, I shall feel so conscious when I meet him, he will divine my secret, and then I should be miserable indeed."

"No, Katie dear, you are too good to be annoyed, and I will promise you that I will say no more about his honor Sir Henry Stuart Vernon, save as a passing acquaintance and friend. There is no doubt we shall be thrown in his way often," said Minnie, "for of course there will be any number of parties given on his account. Each will vie with the other as to who shall show him the greatest attention. You know that it is not often that we are so fortunate as to have an English nobleman at our parties."

"Yes, and I have just thought," I replied, "that he will remember not seeing me at Laura Jenkins's party, and he will ask Arthur the reason, and, of course, the history of our poverty will follow. So here ends my acquaintance with Sir Henry!"

"Nonsense!" said Minnie. "If there is anything to be judged by the looks of a person, Sir Henry will not slight a girl simply because she is poor. I should judge that he thinks there are other treasures in the world beside money."

"Perhaps so," I replied; "but you know, Minnie, that I shall probably not be thrown in his way again. I may be invited to some of the parties; but of course I cannot attend more than two, if any. You know pa will not permit me to wear any of my party-dresses that I wore in my Southern home!

"It seems hard, sometimes, when I think of the elegant silks and satins, with all the other append-ages to a lady's toilette, that are packed away, doing no one any service. Pa says if I wore them it would be a species of deception; and you know he is above every such meanness.

"Ma says that one of these days, when the affairs of the country are settled, that grandpa will send for me to visit him in England, and then I may find them very useful. Grandpa said, in his last letter, that the clouds were breaking, and that, if we did not have trouble on the Alabama question, he thought we may yet recover some of our property that was confiscated.

"As to the parties, my one poor muslin must answer to appear in twice, and that will end my dissipation!"

"And why not three times?" asked Minnie. "You can vary it by using trimmings of a different color and style each time."

"Minnie, you know too well that there will be

some who will sneer, e'en though I wear the dress
for a second time only!"

"I do think," answered Minnie, "that this is one
of the crying evils of the day.

"The useless expenditure, the waste, not only of
time, but of material, in adorning our poor frail
bodies, — and for what?   Surely not to gain the
respect of men, but to gratify pride, — one of the
seven things that the Lord doth hate; to foster
vanity and self-sufficiency!   I know that it is considered almost an insult for a lady to appear at a
party clad in a dress in which she has previously
appeared.

"How many husbands and fathers have been
ruined by this extravagant, foolish custom!   No
wonder so many desirable young men shrink from
the thought of matrimony, when they consider what
it costs to support a family in dress alone.   Is it not
time for some lady of undoubted social position to
introduce reform in this respect?

"I read in last evening's paper that some European princess was about to introduce the fashion
of appearing in plain, unornamented dress, at parties
and assemblies.   But it is a shame for us, who take

the lead in other great works, to allow ourselves to live on in vanity and useless extravagance, till our European sisters initiate the move, and by following which we shall admit their superiority! It is of no use for the women of America to clamor for their *rights*, until they have strength of mind enough to *do* right, independent of the world at large. I, for one, shall rue the day when woman, with her weak and frivolous notions, is admitted to the ballot. I should say, in the words of our good Litany, 'From all *such* evil, good Lord, deliver us!'"

"I don't think you are very complimentary to your sex, Minnie," said I.

"Ah, Kate, you well know that my remarks are just. There are many good, noble, Christian women in our land; but you could not find a single one in the number who would go to the polls, if they were allowed the *privilege* (?).

"It is only poor, vain, conceited, weak-minded women, who writhe under the thought that man is placed by God over them. They are not willing to listen to anything against, what they consider, their rights; but, in the very face of Holy Writ, which expressly declares *man to be the head of woman, she insists on being his equal!* If she cannot gain her end in any other way, she will call in the aid of Satan, and, at last, if the poor men do not receive strength from One *greater* than Satan, they will be so harassed and tormented, that, for the sake of ease and quiet, they will cry, ' *Vote, then,* if this will satisfy you!' But, ah! then it will be too late, when the die is cast; and *woe for our land when woman shall decide its destinies!* Yes, a woe we shall deserve, when men, for their own peace, shall allow women to take a part in our public affairs. Let your women be chaste, — *keepers at home,* not *standing round the polls!* My blood starts at the thought!"

"Why, Minnie," said I, "I really believe you would make another Dickinson; though, judging from appearances, you would be on one side of the hedge, and she on the other."

"The carriage is ready, Miss Manton," said Sam, and, promising to see Minnie at an early day, I bade her good-night, and soon found myself in my humble, but none the less loved home.

VII.

FEBRUARY 23d.

YESTERDAY was Washington's birthday, and, as pa had a holiday, uncle Francis invited us all to visit the former home of Irving. Although the glory of the house was departed, yet a visit to the places once loved and trod by one so universally beloved and admired as Washington Irving, was fraught with the deepest interest.

There had been a slight fall of snow the day previous; but this only added to the beauty of the scenery. The morning was bright and charming. We took the boat up the Hudson, as far as Tarrytown, remarkable for being the place where Andre was captured, and a little to the north of which is "Sleepy Hollow," rendered famous by the legend of Irving. We took a carriage from this place, and drove out to the great author's home.

5

This remarkable man was born in New York city.
He left school at sixteen, and commenced the study
of law. At the age of nineteen he commenced his
literary career, over the signature of "Jonathan
Oldstyle." A year or two after, being afflicted with
pulmonary complaints, he resolved to try the benefit
of a sea voyage, and a visit to the summer climate
of the south of Europe. When he reached Genoa,
he concluded to remain for some weeks in the old
city of palaces.

It was here he first became acquainted with
grandpa, and here that they formed that intimacy
which ended only with life. How I love to hear
grandpa tell about those days! No wonder that he
says they were among the happiest of his life!

I can conceive of nothing more delightful than to
visit places of note in the Old World, that will carry
one far back to the pristine age, with such a man .
as Irving by my side. Genoa is famed, grandpa
says, for its palaces. They are rich in works of
sculpture and painting, as are also the churches
and chapels. Of these last there are about two
hundred and fifty. I can remember the names only
of one or two, — San Lorenzo and San Matteo ; yes,

and Stefano, I think. Grandpa says that the history
of Genoa may be traced back, by tradition, before
the foundation of Rome. Livy mentions it as a
town in friendly relations with the Romans, and in
the time of Strabo it was an emporium for the produce of the interior. When viewed from the harbor,
the city, with its churches, palaces, promenades, and
gardens, the fortifications encircling it, the Apennines,
and the ice-covered peaks of the Alps behind, affords
one of the grandest and most picturesque sights in
the world.

After remaining in Genoa for about two months,
grandpa and Irving visited Naples, and then proceeded to Rome. Naples is in the immediate vicinity
of Vesuvius, and not far from the site. of Herculaneum and Pompeii, and is justly regarded as one
of the most interesting cities in the world, on account
of its classical associations. Its palaces are numerous
and elegant. As you approach it from the sea every
one is struck with its loveliness. I trust the time
will arrive when I shall see for myself, and not be
acquainted with it save by the hearing of the ear!
The streets of the city are straight, and paved with
blocks of lava; but only the principal have side-

walks, or are lighted by gas. The Neapolitans are very fond of out-door life. None, save those of the lowest rank, walk abroad. If they cannot afford a carriage, their pride dooms them to perpetual imprisonment. As the roofs of the houses are flat, they adorn them with flowers and shrubs in boxes, and the care of them afford the women air and exercise.

Nero made his first public appearance on the stage at Naples; but its chief glory was its association with Virgil, who is supposed to have resided there for a considerable time, and whose tomb is said to have been still extant in the time of Statius and Italicus, — which latter poet died in Naples, while the former speaks of the city as his birthplace. In 1860, it was taken possession of by Garibaldi for the King of Sardinia, and, in November, Victor Emanuel entered and took possession of it.

From Naples, grandpa says they proceeded to Rome, where they formed the acquaintance of Washington Allston, which acquaintance, on Irving's part, ripened into intimate friendship. In fact he became so delighted with Italy, that he seriously considered the idea of remaining there, and becoming himself a painter; but, on mature deliberation, he relinquished the thought.

On leaving Rome they proceeded to Paris, where they remained for some time, and at length they landed on England's shore. After remaining there for a short time they returned together to New York, and resumed their law studies, and were duly admitted to the bar. While grandpa gave himself up exclusively to his profession, it seemed to possess no attraction for Irving; his thoughts turned wholly to literature.

After the war of 1812, Irving visited England a second time, where he remained for seventeen years. During this time he visited Scotland, where he became acquainted with Sir Walter Scott.

Scott, in writing to a friend soon after, wrote, " When you see Campbell, tell him, with my best love, that I have to thank him for introducing me to Mr. Washington Irving, who is one of the best and pleasantest acquaintances I have made this many a day !"

Soon after his visit to Scott he met with pecuniary reverses, not, however, owing to any fault of his own, and he was reduced to poverty. It was then

that he wrote his famous "Sketch Book;" and, as
he afterward wrote grandpa, it was to Scott that he
was indebted for his success, as he pronounced it
"positively beautiful!"

After this he filled the post of Minister to Spain
for four years.

For some years before his death he resided at
"Sunnyside," the beautiful spot that we visited yesterday. This is on the banks of the Hudson, near
by "Sleepy Hollow," of which place he says, "If
ever I should wish for a retreat where I might steal
from the world and its distractions, and dream
quietly away the remainder of a troubled life, I
know of none more promising than this little valley."

The house at "Sunnyside" is the identical dwelling represented as the castle of Baltus Von Tassel,
where Ichabod Crane paid his addresses to the little
Dutch beauty Katrina, and in which the great country
frolic took place. It is a poet's cottage, lost in ver-
dure and flowers, nestling down on the banks of that
beautiful river, which the master of the mansion
has adorned and illustrated by his genius. The
house is in the genuine Dutch style, and everything
about it is redolent of bygone days.

Here, on the banks of this beautiful stream, away from the world and its distraction, as he had wished, did the loved Irving tranquilly pass his last years.

Uncle Francis says that he was never married. He told grandpa that he had loved a beautiful lady by the name of Hoffman, and that he intended to marry her; but she died, and he had no room in his heart for a second love!

When he lay upon his death-bed he had her Bible, — an old and time-worn copy, — on a table by his side. His brothers and their children made a happy home for him, as uncle Francis and grandpa can aver, for they visited him often. He died of heart disease, about ten years since. Uncle Francis was at his funeral. He says that the procession passed by a road which winds through " Sleepy Hollow ; " and near that place, rendered famous by his genius, he now sleeps.

On our return home we visited his grave, and left our tribute behind, — a tear! for ours was not the admiration of genius alone, but love for the man. He was our friend. Many were the days and weeks that he had passed at grandpa's, where he had endeared himself to all our hearts. Of none of those who have been classed among our friends do I feel more proud, than of the friendship of Washington Irving. A small lock of his hair, and a copy of his " Sketch Book," containing my name, written in his own valued handwriting, are among my most precious mementos!

When we arrived home, which was not till after nine o'clock, I found two cards bearing the names of Vernon and Jenkins! I must confess the truth, and say that I was perfectly crestfallen at first, for Sir Henry had called upon us but once before, and I had really brought myself to believe that the sight of our humble home would keep his lordship from calling a second time.

What could have prompted him? I have never met him at an evening party, for the simple reason that I have never attended one; although, to my great surprise, I have received an invitation to every one, with the exception of two, that has been given this winter. It is well!

Our depression in circumstances is producing a good effect upon me.

I am beginning to see that " this world is but a fleeting show, for man's illusion given; " every day brings some fresh token of its selfishness and vanity. But I must try by my actions to show, and not only to show, but to *be* a child of wisdom in this evil generation. I must study my Bible more, and learn to be like Christ, my Saviour, who was poor for my sake. I must try to be patient. I must be willing to suffer evil, and, what is harder than all, to *think* no evil.

What a world this would be if that charity which the Bible teaches us, "That vaunteth not itself, — that is not puffed up," should be practised by all men.

Well! I will try, for one, and cultivate the spirit, and perhaps others will follow my example.

And now, instead of disquieting myself about the notice and opinions of others, I will commence at once a course of study, and revive at least all my historical knowledge; for if grandpa should send for me to go out to England, I should not wish to feel myself an ignoramus, knowing nothing of England as a country, or of its inhabitants as a people; and while I think of it, I will purchase a manuscript this afternoon, which I will devote exclusively to general information regarding all the countries of Europe, —

their principal localities, kings and queens, — great men, aye, and women too! But the first and most important thing is to acquaint myself at once with the names and lineage of the *present* kings and queens, for I must confess that I am deplorably ignorant on this subject. I fear if Sir Henry should introduce any of them as a topic of conversation, he would think I ought to attend school again at once.

It is really sad to think that as soon as a young lady leaves school, and goes into society, how soon its vanities and vexations will cause her to forget almost all she ever did learn. But there's the dinner-bell again. It doesn't seem more than an hour since breakfast; but I must run, as pa very much dislikes tardiness.

MARCH 1st.

Last evening I attended what was declared to be the most elegant party of the season, at Mrs. Luddington's.

Her husband was a classmate of grandpa's, and while in college formed an intimacy with him which has never yet been interrupted.

Mr. Luddington is an old-school gentleman, dignified, yet courteous in his bearing, with a face so full of sympathy and kindness that even a child would love him.

Mrs. Luddington, like her husband, although an elegant, most highly-accomplished lady, has a soul overflowing with love and good-will to all, and never is her high breeding more manifest than in her efforts to show that she esteems others better than herself!

I wore my white muslin, — my first appearance in it, — trimmed in the plainest manner with folds of lace, and silk of the palest blue; not a jewel of any kind, although I must confess to a little chagrin when I thought of the elegant set of pearls, — necklace, bracelets, pin and ear-rings, my last gift from grandpa before the horrid war, — lying packed away in my escritoire at home, doing service to none.'

But then pa said it would be highly improper for me to wear them; and, in fact, on a little reflection I thought so too! A few snow-berries, just peeping from among their green leaves, were the only decoration to my hair; a small silver cross, a gift from Minnie, was my pin: kid gloves of the palest blue, black satin slippers, and white silk stockings, — remnants of my better days, — one of my simplest embroidered handkerchiefs, with just a drop of "Love among the Roses," and an exquisite little fan of rice, sent me by a gentleman from France in my younger days.

As almost every one, however poor, has some such trinket, which, if not presented to them personally, descended from their ancestors, pa thought it not amiss that I should take it. I have a weakness in this particular. I always feel more at ease if I can find some way in which to employ my hands while at a party!

Minnie called for me just before nine; it is so thoughtful in her. It is not every girl who would be willing to call in her own carriage to convey one to a party who cannot afford to *hire* one for the purpose, much less ride in her own!

While we were arranging ourselves in the dressing-room, preparatory to descending to the drawing-room, Minnie spoke of my appearance. She assured me that "I looked lovely, and that the most fastidious person present could find no fault with me. My dress was plain, but in perfect taste." This she said not to flatter me, but to reassure me, and I was much more at ease for her kind approval, as I knew she was sincere.

Minnie Maverick is a girl that one can trust. She is not of that class of women who are all things to all men! She would *scorn* the thought of praising one's appearance to their face, and making sport of them as soon as they had turned away! Minnie is a girl of character and heart. If she knows her duty, she tries to perform it. She never asks, as weak-minded people ever do, " What will this one say?" or " What will that one think?" She has a mind of her own ; and, though possessed of a large organ of approbativeness, never sacrifices her own independence to the whims and caprice of others.

Minnie looked very handsomely. Her dress was of rich blue silk, — an overskirt of white silk tissue, trimmed with a deep puffing around the bottom, and three garlands of blue flowers passing around the back part of the dress, raising the tissue in puffs that form panniers. A string of pearls were around her hair, pearl pin and ear-rings, gloves that matched the dress in shade, and a handsome bouquet in an elegant silver flower-holder!

Mr. Maverick entertains the same opinion that pa does; and that is, a strong dislike for a lady, under any circumstances, exposing her arms and neck at an evening party; consequently Minnie and I belong to the high-neck and long-sleeve class!

As we entered the drawing-room, young Fred Luddington, who was standing near the door as we entered, offered me his arm, and Harry Hamilton offering his to Minnie; we were led up to pay our respects to the host and hostess.

We then joined a group of young ladies who were busily engaged in discussing some subject, which we learned to be as to the presence of Sir Henry Vernon.

A distinguished Englishman is a lion in our set. Nothing creates so intense an excitement as the arrival of a foreigner, especially if he is distingué! Suddenly the voices subsided into a gentle murmur; and as I turned my head to learn the cause, I saw Sir Henry, with Laura Jenkins hanging on his arm, and Arthur Jenkins, with Emily Schuyler, just paying their devoirs to Mr. and Mrs. Luddington.

Breathe not my weakness! but I felt for a moment, — just a moment, — as if bereft of sense and feeling! By the time they had approached our group, I was perfectly self-possessed, though I imagine I looked a trifle pale. Sir Henry bowed very politely, and passed on, Laura still hanging on his arm. The criticisms now fell fast and thick, but *they* passed on and heard them not. *I* heard them.

"They say," said Belle Schuyler, "that Vernon and Laura Jenkins are to make a match. Charlie says that Arthur brought him over simply on Laura's account."

"I don't think much of Englishmen, any way," said Fanny Hamilton; "for my own part I am very well contented with our New Yorkers, although I have a strong penchant for Southern gentlemen; but if they are American they are all one, or *ought* to be!"

"I don't believe Mr. Vernon has a thought of any one this side of the Atlantic," said Minnie, "for I have good reason to think he left his heart on the other side."

"Not his heart!" said Harry Hamilton, — oh! how I thanked him, — "for report says that his hand only is promised; his heart goes not with it."

"I dare say there are scores of young ladies present who would not care a straw for his heart, if they could only secure his hand," said Belle Schuyler. "Not one in ten, in this age, *believe* in love, or hearts."

"I hope you don't judge by yourself, Miss Schuyler," said Harry Hamilton, mischievously.

"Ah, no, Mr. Hamilton!" And Belle, affecting a sigh, but speaking from her heart more than she would desire us to suspect, said, in a low whisper, —

> "A home in the heart is a home for me,
> Whether it be on land or sea!"

We were amused at the sly glances that passed between her and Harry..

"Well," said Grace Montague, "I for one must say that I am rather glad I have not, as yet, made Mr. Vernon's acquaintance; for I should be in continual terror lest he should say something in regard to England that I should know nothing about, and I verily believe I should die of mortification!

"I am sorry to say that a continual round of parties, theatres, and like dissipation, in the winter, with Newport, and its round of fashionable society, in the summer, has so completely engrossed my thoughts and time, that I have just about forgotten all my former knowledge of history.

"I used to be quite a proficient in that study, and had the names of all the kings and queens, with their right of succession, dates of birth, marriage and death, at my tongue's end; but when one leaves school, and goes into society, there are so many things to distract the attention, that, without method and effort, one's education is almost thrown away."

Just at this moment, Mr. Vernon, who had disengaged himself from Laura, joined our group. He was formally introduced to Misses Montague, Hamilton, and Schuyler, whom he recognized as having been in society with him, but to whom he had not had the pleasure of an introduction.

"I really think, Mr. Vernon, your visit to America will conduce highly to the improvement of some of our young ladies," said Belle Schuyler.

"In what respect, may I ask?" said Sir Henry, smiling.

Poor Grace Montague looked unutterable things.

"I can answer for myself," said Belle, "that I

6

have been very much afraid lest you may introduce, in conversation, some Englishman of renown, of whom I may have been so unfortunate as never to have heard, and, even though I may have been familiar with his history in days gone by, that I may have forgotten. So I will now inform you that I remember scarcely anything concerning English history, and you will not be disappointed in me. I can just recall William the Silent, William Rufus, and Edward the Black Prince ; also Bloody Mary, Elizabeth, and Anne Boleyn. These I cannot forget ; but as to the Georges, — the Hanoverian line, — the houses of York and Lancaster, — as far as I am concerned, they rest in the tomb of the Capulets!"

"I will give you credit for candor, most certainly," said Mr. Vernon ; "and as to your historical knowledge, I presume if any of your American gentlemen should visit England, they would find a large number of English ladies, who consider themselves highly educated, as unfamiliar with the history of America as you are with England. I myself heard one of them remark, in the presence of a number of gentlemen and ladies, that the Americans were a conceited, *puny* race !

"I answered that they were anything but *puny;* for in their infancy they whipped their old mother England so severely, she would retain her scars till the day of her death.

"The young lady was astonished, and had not the slightest recollection of any such event.

"I assured her that it would be much better for us, as a nation, to *remember* it, and to be very careful that we never again irritated so powerful a people.

"But, Miss Schuyler, I must say that I think, not only here, but in the Old World, there is not time enough given to the cultivation of the memory and the mind. No matter of how much knowledge a man may be possessed, he must be constantly reviewing and increasing it, or it will gradually fade from his mind. I think if every young gentleman and lady should set aside a portion of time for each day, and devote themselves to acquiring general information, thereby preventing the current of thought from growing stagnant, there would not be so much folly and worldly-mindedness laid to their charge."

"I agree with you perfectly, Mr. Vernon," said Minnie, "and, I doubt not, all my friends will unite with me in thanking you for your advice, and in endeavoring to profit by it."

Of course we all nodded in acquiescence.

"But it is so difficult, after you have formed a plan, to keep to it," said Grace Montague. "It is almost impossible, in this frivolous age, to fix your attention on the more serious side of life."

"Try it, Miss Montague," said Mr. Vernon; "I hardly believe you will continue to think it a serious side, but I think, in a short time, if you persevere with it, you will anticipate it as one of your most enjoyable hours!"

Just then the sound of music struck upon our ears, and the crowd commenced moving toward the spot. As Sir Henry was standing nearest me, of course he offered me his arm; common politeness could have done no less. He said, in a low tone, "that he regretted not finding me at home on the evening of his call."

I answered that "I equally regretted being absent from home, but that I had gone on an excursion with my parents and uncle, to visit the home of Washington Irving."

I did not tell him that Irving was a friend of

grandpa's. I had just pride enough left to feel that if Sir Henry was my friend, he must be so on account of myself, and not because I was the granddaughter of a judge! Neither did I glance at him to see how he was affected by the mention of the name of *Irving!*

" How much I should have enjoyed being of your party, Miss Manton!" said he.

" I should have been most happy to have had you accompany us, had I have been aware that it would have afforded you any pleasure," I replied.

" I think this is the first party at which I have had the pleasure of meeting you, Miss Manton."

" It is the first one of this season which I have attended," I replied; and, with some hesitancy, I added, " I attend only one or two in a season; my father's means will not allow of my attending more."

" And can you witness the beauty and elegance attendant upon these parties once or twice only, and remain contented during the remainder of the season?" he inquired.

" Better now than formerly," I replied. " It was very hard at first, I admit; but, as time progresses, it is much easier to endure the trial. My allowing myself to be unhappy would be of no avail, and would enhance greatly the unhappiness of my parents. I take for my lesson each day, to ' be content with such things as I have.' "

Our conversation was beginning to attract the notice of the surrounders; which, as Mr. Vernon observed, he very kindly left me with Minnie, and withdrew to another part of the room; not, however, until he had given me another glance into his heart! I strove to pay attention to the music; I answered Minnie's look of inquiry with an amused smile; and how could I help it? To be obliged to hear what I would fain have shut my ears against, — the remarks that were made at my expense. " A *drawing*-teacher ! " " Poor ! " " Lives in a small, out-of-the-way place in Harlem ! " " Her father was a *rebel!* Just good enough for them; always thinking themselves better than their neighbors ! " " These Southern nabobs do feel so big, even if they are poor as church-mice ! " I was greatly amused. The very idea of their being jealous and envious of me, who feel myself less than the least among them! Poor deluded mortals! I had vastly rather be slandered than the slanderer!

Shortly after, supper was announced. Sir Henry took Mrs. Luddington to the supper-room; and, to my great surprise, Mr. Luddington took poor, insignificant me! It is surprising how an attention like this will sometimes call into being emotions of a strength and nature that remain during life. How grateful, when one conceives herself to be the least, to receive such attention. Had I have been the Duchess of Sutherland, I could not have been treated with more marked consideration or respect.

The repast, of course, was sumptuous, and served in the most magnificent style. Mrs. Luddington embraced the opportunity to ask me about grandpa, and evinced so great an interest in everything concerning us, that I really felt quite at ease.

Whether it was the particular attention shown me by the host and hostess, or from the promptings of his own heart, I cannot say; but one thing is true, — that Sir Henry asked the honor of escorting me to my carriage, when it should arrive; and from that moment till the carriage was announced, I scarcely knew whether I was in or out of the body!

Kate Manton, where are your fine resolves never again to think of Sir Henry Vernon? Take the warnings of your own heart, and do not deceive yourself into a belief that he cares for you, save as he may care for any valued friend! Rest assured you will save yourself much pain if you will follow these promptings.

> "Others love, are loved, filled full thereof;
> I, only I, must faint and fall;
> Must starve for that I can never have! ah me!"

VIII.

LAURA JENKINS called yesterday, and I must say, in justice to her, she appears lovely. What a rival I have in her! handsome, wealthy, and accomplished, — while I am poor, plain, and good-natured only because I have to be! I very much fear, at times, that if the few friends I possess could look into my heart, and see it just as it is, I should number fewer still.

Laura made a very handsome apology for not inviting me to her party, and then invited me to take a trip on the Hudson, as far as West Point, the following day. Thanking her for her kindness, I assured her I would accept the invitation with the greatest pleasure.

And now, as it is but five o'clock, and we do not start till nine, I will try and refresh my memory so far as the present kings and queens of Europe are

concerned, so that I may feel a little at ease if Sir
Henry should chance to engage me in conversation, — for, of course, he will be there! and Minnie,
— dear girl that she is, — she will keep me in countenance, at least. Let me see, — yes, I will begin
with Victoria : —

Victoria Alexandrina, Queen of Great Britain
and Ireland, born at Kensington Palace, May 24th,
1819. She is the daughter of Edward, Duke of
Kent, fourth son of George the Third, and the Princess Victoria Mary Louisa of Saxe Coburg Saalfeld.
Her father died in 1820; and, as neither George the
Fourth, nor his brothers next of kin, — the Dukes
of York and Clarence, — had surviving children,
she was looked upon as future sovereign of England.

On the death of George the Fourth he was succeeded by his brother, the Duke of Clarence, who
received the name of William Henry from his uncle,
the Duke of Gloucester, and ascended the throne in
1830, with the title of William the Fourth. As he
died without a male heir, it caused the crown of
Hanover to be separated from that of Great Britain,
— his brother, the Duke of Cumberland, becoming

King of Hanover, and his niece, Victoria, Queen of Great Britain. She was therefore crowned in Westminster Abbey, June 28th, 1838, and in August, 1859, she was also proclaimed Queen of Hindostan.

On February 10th, 1840, Victoria married Prince Albert of Saxe Coburg Gotha, who died December 14th, 1861, — the same year of the death of her mother, the Duchess of Kent.

Victoria has had nine children, — Victoria Adelaide, who married the Crown Prince of Prussia, — Albert Edward, Prince of Wales, who married Alexandrina, Princess of Denmark, — Alice, who married Prince Louis of Hesse, — Alfred, Helena, Louisa, Arthur, Leopold, and Beatrice.

Louis Charles Napoleon Bonaparte is the present Emperor of the French. He was the youngest son of Louis Bonaparte, King of Holland, and Hortense Beauharnais, the daughter of the Empress Josephine, and consequently nephew of the great Napoleon! He was born in Paris, in 1808.

After Louis Philippe was dethroned, he was chosen deputy to the National Assembly, and when in 1850 the election for President came on, he was found to

be the most popular candidate, and was chosen by
a large majority of votes. Before two years had
transpired, a decree was put forth ordering the establishment of universal suffrage, and the election
of a President for ten years. He was, of course,
elected under this decree. At the close of 1852, the
people were asked to revive the imperial dignity in
the person of Louis Napoleon. The votes were
largely in his favor, and he was declared Emperor,
under the title of Napoleon Third.

In 1853 he married Eugénie, Countess de Teba,
a Spanish lady of remarkable beauty and accomplishments. He has one son, born in 1856. He succeeded Louis Philippe, who ascended the throne of
France in 1830, from the branch known as Bourbon
Orleans, tracing its origin to Philippe, Duke of
Orleans. Louis Philippe reigned eighteen years,
and lost his crown in the revolution of February, 1848.

Francis Joseph, the reigning Emperor of Austria,
was the eldest son of the Archduke Francis Charles,
and the Archduchess Sophia, daughter of the King
of Bavaria, and sister of the Queens of Prussia and
Saxony.

He was also grandson of Francis Second, Emperor of Germany, and First, of Austria, whom he succeeded. He was nephew of Ferdinand First, and also of Maria Louisa, second wife of the great Napoleon. He was born in 1830. In 1854 he married Elizabeth, daughter of the Bavarian Duke Maximilian Joseph of Zwerbrücken Birkenfeld. Francis First, the grandfather of the present Emperor, was the son of Leopold Second, and of Maria Louisa, daughter of Charles Third, King of Spain; and Francis Charles, the father of the present Emperor, was his son by his second wife, Maria Theresa.

William First, King of Prussia, is the second son of Frederic William the Third. He was born in 1797, and succeeded his brother Frederic William Fourth to the throne in 1861, and was crowned at Konigsberg. He was married in 1829 to the Duchess Marie Luise Auguste Katharine, of Saxe Weimar. He had a son and daughter — the elder, the Crown Prince Friedrich Wilhelm Nicholas Karl, born in 1831, married in 1858, to Victoria, Princess Royal of Great Britain; and the younger, the Princess Luise

Marie Elizabeth, born in 1838, and married in 1856, to the Grand Duke Frederic of Baden.

Alexander Second, Czar of Russia, was born in 1818.   He was the son and successor of Nicholas First.   His mother was Charlotte of Prussia, the eldest daughter of Frederic William the Third.

In 1841 he married Maria Alexandrowna, Grand Duchess of Hesse Darmstadt.   It was wholly a love match, the young prince having made his own choice among a host of German princesses.   He ascended the throne in 1855.   Alexander is the eldest of five children; his sister Maria, next in age, is widow of the Duke of Leuchtenburg; Olga, wife of the Crown Prince of Wurtemburg, Nicholas, and Michael.

I cannot say how much of these I shall remember, but my memory is certainly refreshed a little.   How foolish we young ladies are to waste so much time in frivolous pursuits!   Why can we not think more of the mind, and strive to cultivate that?

Learning is *always* respected.   No matter what a man's social position, if he is educated, and we find that he is our superior in literary attainments, the knowledge at once elicits our respect.

Not that I approve of being a bookworm, or a blue-stocking, but there is a happy medium in this as in all things.

Would each young lady devote one hour in the morning, before breakfast, instead of wasting that precious time in bed, to the study of some useful subject, a new era would dawn upon us! It is melancholy to find how much ignorance lies concealed beneath the chignons, crimps, curls and velvets, to say nothing of the imperials, mustaches, and whiskers of our youth! Verily, all is vanity! Ah! here is Minnie, and I must array myself for the excursion.

MARCH 3d.

Such a glorious time as I had yesterday! We had a pleasant party of twenty, — twelve ladies and eight gentlemen. Minnie and I were escorted by Arthur Jenkins, and Laura, with Emily Schuyler, were under Sir Henry Vernon's escort, at least when we started. I am not at all jealous of Laura. It seems as if Sir Henry belongs to her by right. I was calm and self-possessed, although I confess to an indescribable trembling when he first lifted his hat and bowed to me! But I am growing wiser; yes! wiser.

What difference will it make to me whom I love, or who loves me, when fifty years shall have rolled their round? What difference, when I leave this world, with all its vanities, to go hence, and be known no more, whether I am married or single, rich or poor, envied or despised?

None! If Christ will give me strength to walk in just such paths as He approves; to follow, not the inclination of my own sinful heart, but after that which is well-pleasing in His sight, — if *He* is my friend, it is enough!

It was a glorious morning! Crowds of people were standing on the wharves. The steamer, which was ready to start as soon as we were on board, lay at the foot of the pier.

As we passed on to the boat, I was very much delighted by meeting Judge Francis, a chum of grandpa's, in old Harvard.

He is a fine-looking, elderly gentleman of the old school, and had with him his wife and daughter.

They were returning from a visit in Washington, to their home in Newburg; were very cordial, and gave me an urgent invitation to visit them in their home.

"I hear, Kate, how nobly you are bearing your reverses!" said the Judge. "They will do you no harm, but will develop your character and mind, and I doubt not you will yet live to thank the Lord for leading you by this very way."

"Oh," I replied, "please don't praise me, sir; for I bear it anything but nobly. I am easily irritated, and prone to be very bitter against those who dare look down upon me; and yet I suppose it is perfectly natural that some weak minds should feel thus; for they know that I am a hated Southerner!

"You know, sir, there are a great many at the North who believe that in a Southerner there is no good thing!"

"Ah," said the Judge, "you must not feel thus, Miss Kate. I think, now that Grant is in the Presidential chair, this feeling will be done away with in a great measure."

"Excuse me for disagreeing with you, sir; but I think if our noble Seymour had have been elected, we should have had a much better chance of being restored to our true position as Southerners. My father is with you, sir; but ma and I are filled with sympathy for the Democratic cause; and the one redeeming feature only in 'Woman's Rights,' — the right of the *ballot*, — is, that when *that* day shall arrive, there will be no struggle between parties; for the women will carry in the Democratic candidate with such an overpowering majority, there will be no necessity for the poor Republicans to present a candidate!"

"Well, really, Miss Kate, you are quite a politician; but if I thought there was the least ground for your suspicions, I should wield my pen with all its force against 'Woman's Rights'! Why, Miss Kate, if the Democrats should be again in power, the country would be ruined!"

"It is laughable," I replied, "how conceited you Republicans are;" and then, remembering how superior Judge Francis was to me in age as well as intellect, I said, "You will pardon me, sir, I did not intend being rude, but I do feel that we, as a part of the country, are *so* wronged!

" I feel that I am becoming, however, more recon-
ciled to my fate, and I trust. it will make of me a
more perfect woman ! "

I then invited Miss Francis to walk to another
part of the boat, and allow me to introduce her to
my friends.

She politely acceded to my request.

I felt proud of the honor of introducing her. She
was an elegant young lady, of about twenty-six,
dressed in the most perfect taste, with an air of
high-breeding that betokened the lady. Shortly
after her introduction, Mr. Vernon asked me " if
Miss Francis, whose name was very familiar, was a
relative of Judge Francis, formerly of New York?'

" She is his daughter," I replied.

" I then asked him if he was acquainted with
Judge Francis? "

" Only by reputation," he replied.

" He was an intimate friend of my uncle Sir
Albert Vernon, in years gone by."

After a moment's hesitation, he asked me " if I
would favor him with an introduction to the Judge?"
and as I cordially assented, he gave me his arm,

and we walked to the part of the boat where Judge
Francis and his wife were sitting.

When I mentioned Sir Henry's name, the Judge
started, and exclaimed, "Is it possible? Do I indeed behold the nephew of my valued friend Sir
Albert Fortescue Vernon? I think I must have
recognized you by your strong resemblance to your
uncle. And your father?"

"Was Sir Henry Stuart Vernon!"

"Yes, I knew him also; but not as intimately as
his brother. It is many years since I heard of or
from your uncle."

"He has been a confirmed invalid," Sir Henry
replied, "for nearly ten years."

"Your grandfather, Kate, Judge Blake, was
another friend of Sir Henry's uncle."

"Your *grandfather*, Miss Manton!" said Sir
Henry. "Wonders will never cease! Why, I
have dined at my uncle's, with your grandfather,
within six months!

"Why did I not know of your relationship? I
have asked Arthur of your relatives, Miss Kate;"
and then, with a blush, as if he had unnecessarily
committed himself, he added, "your face reminded

me so strongly of one I had seen before, and this accounts for it.

"Arthur told me simply that you were a Southerner; once in high social life, but now suffering adversity, caused by your dreadful war!

"Ah, Arthur," said Sir Henry, aside, "I did not think this of you.

"I have evinced more interest in Miss Manton than I ought, and it may be that you fear Laura will have a rival, — poor fellow! I have not lived these years for nothing, and in future I will be more careful to guard my secret; therefore I will assume an air of nonchalance with all."

"And so, Miss Manton, Judge Blake is your grandfather?"

"He was my mother's father," I replied.

"Yes; and Miss Manton's father would have been a Judge by this time, had it not have been for the horrible war!"

"Splendid talents! splendid talents, I assure you, Mr. Vernon," said the Judge, "but obliged to come North and take a position with the paltry sum of fourteen hundred a year; and this young lady, who is his blessing — " but I excused myself, and joined our party, knowing full well that Judge Francis would leave nothing unsaid in my favor.

And now we drew near the place where the Hudson begins its passage through the beautiful hills called the "Highlands," which rise abruptly from the water; while, in some places, vessels following the channel pass so near the shore that one can almost touch the cliffs from their decks.

Among the most remarkable of these hills are Beacon, — so named from the signal fires which used to burn on its summit during the Revolutionary War, — "Crow's Nest," "Sugar Loaf Mountain," "Anthony's Nose," and "Dunderberg," — the "Thunder Chamber," as it is called.

Instead of stopping at West Point, we concluded to enjoy the sail as far as Newburg, and take the return boat for West Point.

As Newburg broke upon our view I was perfectly delighted with its appearance. There it rose in its beauty, on a steep slope, rising, as Judge Francis informed us, to a height of somewhere about one hundred and fifty feet, on the west bank of the Hudson. There stood the court-house, — of which Judge Francis was the Superior Judge, — large manufactories, foundries, and the spires of nearly twenty churches, which I counted. The Judge informed us that that they were supplied with water from " Little Pond," which was about three miles distant.

He also pointed out an old stone mansion which overlooked the Hudson, which, he said, was " Washington's Headquarters," and which was owned and kept in order by the State. Besides its association with the Revolutionary War, and its great Chief, the building contains numerous interesting relics of that period.

When the boat stopped, the Judge and his family repeated their cordial invitation to visit them in Newburg, and extended the invitation also to all our party to pass a day, and visit the old stone mansion and any other objects of interest.

Sir Henry escorted them to the wharf. Stop, my miserably jealous heart!

Do you see a rival in Miss Francis also?

Anything but a *jealous* young lady!

I pity the man who weds her, — and yet there is much of it in woman's nature!

She hates to see the man she loves showing interest in any other; and yet if he objects to her flirting (just for *fun* you know *her* flirtations are, with Tom, Richard, and Henry), she is *so* injured, — he begins to think he is the aggressor rather than the aggrieved! Oh, what a compound women are! allowing themselves in things that if their poor husbands ever *dreamed* of even, they would find no rest for their poor souls!

We enjoyed the extended trip greatly; and on our return between Newburg and West Point, we dined on board the boat, that we may devote all the time that remained in seeing the "lions" at West Point.

In the midst of the "Highlands," to which I have before alluded, where the Hudson flows with so many windings, which add so greatly to its beauty, on a bold promontory, commanding magnificent views both North and South, stands West Point.

This was an important fortress during the Revolutionary War, but its chief importance is in its being the seat of the United States Military Academy.

Near by stands Mount Independence, about a mile to the south-west, on the crest of which, in the Revolution, stood Fort Putnam, surrounded on three sides by deep ravines commanding the river, and protecting the other defences. It stood between five and six hundred feet above the river.

Another fort, called " Clinton," stood on the northeast side. Most of the works were built under the superintendence of Kosciusko. I remembered the treason of Arnold consisted in obtaining command of the fortress by false representations, with the intention of surrendering it to the British, — which scheme was happily foiled by André's arrest.

On landing at West Point we turned our steps toward the Military Academy. The buildings are of stone; one, nearly three hundred feet long, is designed for military exercise in the winter. There is also a fine building of Gothic architecture, with towers for astronomical apparatus, — the middle tower revolving for an observatory, — which we visited. Connected with the Academy is the chapel, hospital, magazine, soldiers' barracks, and other things too numerous to mention.

The instruction in the Academy is free; but the cadet, unless released by government, is required to serve the country eight years after finishing his course:

I always thought that any one who had a taste for military life, could enter there and fit himself for it; but I learned that every one who enjoyed its advantages as a member of the Academy, must be chosen either by Congress or the President.

How time flies! Before we had time to visit any other part of the place, Mr. Jenkins said we must start for the quay, as the boat would be there in about ten minutes.

Mr. Vernon escorted me to the landing, and said if I should be disengaged the following evening, he would do himself the honor to call!

Of course I replied that I had no engagement whatever, and that I should be very happy to see him.

And here it is almost tea-time; so I will run down and dust the parlor, and add a little water to my flowers, and then dress. Shall I powder just a little? No! I have said that I wouldn't, and I will not, let the consequence be what it will. I wish, however, I had not been quite so rash in promising, as I should like to look brilliant, if such a thing is possible! But it cannot be, and Sir Henry must take me just as I am.

But first, let me reassure myself on the present European sovereigns.

I remember well, — Victoria, Napoleon, Francis Joseph, William First, and Alexander Second. I must know a little more of the principal ones, certainly, even if I go without my tea. I *will* not be so ignorant! There is —

Isabella Second, Queen of Spain, who has so lately abdicated the throne, fled into France, and taken up an elegant abode in Paris; her first abode being the chateau in which Henry the Fourth of France was born, and from which there is a magnificent view of the Pyrenees, while Spain is in a state of revolution. She was the daughter of Ferdinand Seventh, King of Spain (who died in Madrid in 1833, and who was the son of Charles Fourth and Luisa Maria of Parma), and his fourth wife, Maria Christina, daughter of King Francis of Naples. Isabella was a child of little more than three years of age when she ascended the throne, which she obtained by her father's repealing the Salic law, introduced into Spain by Philip Fifth, and naming Isabella to succeed him, thus excluding his brother,

Don Carlos, who was heir presumptive by virtue of that law. In 1846 she married her cousin, Don Francisco de Assiz, Duke of Cadiz, and son of Francisco de Paula, brother of Ferdinand Seventh.

When the Spanish throne was overthrown, in 1868, those who took possession of the government resolved to call a Congress, and arranged that the members of this Congress should be chosen by the votes of the Spaniards, from twenty-five upward.

Victor Emanuel, King of Italy, was born in 1820, and is the eldest son of Charles Albert and Theresa, daughter of the late Grand Duke Ferdinand of Tuscany.

He has five children, — Clotilda, wife of Prince Napoleon Jerome; Humbert, Prince of Piedmont; Amadeus, Duke of Aosta; Otho, Duke of Montferrat; and Maria Pia.

Twenty years ago he was king only of Sardinia, while the rest of the country was under the control of the Pope, the house of Bourbon, and the Austrians, as well as of lesser sovereigns, — the Grand Duke of Tuscany, the Duke of Modena, and the Duke of Parma.

Now he is King of Italy; and his kingdom in-
cludes the entire peninsula except a small part under
the Pope, and the island of Sicily.

In acquiring Italy he adopted Napoleon Third's
practice of referring different political questions to
the inhabitants of the country; and, by this suffrage,
the Tuscans, Sicilians, Neapolitans, and Romagnese
decided to become his subjects.

The revolution which effected this, in 1861, was
directed by Garibaldi, accompanied by whom Victor
Emanuel entered Naples in triumph, and was declared King of Italy. But the feelings of the people
toward the King are undergoing a great change.

The Italian Parliament is holding a stormy session.

The grist-mill tax has caused serious disturbance.
The mills are closed; the peasants have ceased their
labors, and march in procession, uttering seditious
cries. They have sacked the palaces, poured out
the wine from the wine-shops, and resisted the troops
sent to disperse them. The country is quiet now;
but the tax, although small, is felt to be grievous.
Italy is passing through another crisis in her history.

John, King of Saxony, son of the Duke Max-

110 MAN'S WRONGS;

imilian and the Princess of Parma, was born in 1801, and succeeded his brother Frederic Augustus in 1854. His wife is a daughter of Maximilian of Bavaria.

His eldest daughter married the Duke of Genoa, a brother of the King of Sardinia, who died in 1855. His eldest son, Frederic Augustus Albert, married a daughter of Prince Gustavus Vasa.

William Third, King of the Netherlands, succeeded his father, William Second. He was born in 1817, educated in England, and married in 1839 the Princess Sophia of Wurtemburg. In 1849 he ascended the throne. He has two sons, William Prince of Orange, born in 1840, and Prince Alexander, born in 1851. And beside all these, there are —

Charles Fifteenth, King of Norway and Sweden; *Christian Ninth*, King of Denmark; *Louis*, King of Portugal; *Louis Second*, King of Bavaria; *Leopold Second*, King of Belgium; *Frederic*, Grand Duke of Baden; *Charles First*, King of Wurtemburg; *George First*, King of Hellenes; *Charles*, Prince of Roumania, and *Abdul Aziz Khan*, Sultan of Turkey.

If I can remember the names of the kings over

these smaller kingdoms, it will be all I can do at present.

Dear me, it is six o'clock, and I have done nothing, scarcely. How my heart beats as the time draws near for Sir Henry to make his appearance!

IX.

L AST evening, as soon as I had supped, I ran up stairs and read over a few times the names of the kings and queens which I had selected, when the thought occurred, — but who are some of the great men and women of the past as well as the present age?

To think of any but Scott and Shakespeare I could not; and though I blush to own it, I knew but little more of these than the name!

Tell it not in Gath, for I really considered myself quite a finished young lady. This will *never* do, thought I. I must turn over a new leaf at once, rise up early in the morning, and see if I cannot acquire such information as will enable me to be something more than an ignoramus, in my own estimation at least! If I can only remember some of our *own* great men, it will be better than nothing; but so many of them are Northerners that I never felt much interest in them, to tell the truth, though I must own to admiring the writings, if not the men!

There are Longfellow and Whittier; yes! and Webster and Everett. I admire these last two; for *Webster!* isn't he the *greatest* statesman that America ever produced? and Everett — didn't ma and I tease pa to vote for him and our own loved Bell? Yes! and he would not do it, even to please us!

Now if the women could have voted *then*, there would have been no war, and I should not be living in Harlem!

But then I should never have seen Sir Henry, — so I suppose it is all for the best that the women *can't* vote; for they would surely be putting themselves in office.

Then there is Mrs. Stowe — I suppose they call *her* a great woman! I do not see why! It was not the story itself of poor uncle Tom that was so superior, but the writing it *just at that time*, when all the Northerners were so anxious to cast out their Southern brothers' mote, that they did not see their own beam! They were almost insane upon the theme of Slavery; and when this book appeared to

8

fan the flame already kindled into a fire, and to make
men believe that every one of us Southerners were
abusing our poor blacks, — when there is hardly one
among us who would *begin* to treat our slaves as
they treat the poor among them, — they fall upon the
book with such enthusiasm as to enroll its writer
among the names of the greatest writers of the
age!

I will admit, however, that she must have a stronger
head than most women, or it would be turned by such
adulation! As everybody says she is *great*, I suppose what everybody says must be true!

Then there is Beecher! I must say, after all, if
I *am* a Southerner, I like Beecher! I wish we
could afford to sit under his preaching.

But it is with this, as with everything else: those
who are blessed with money, have a host of other
blessings. They can hear the best preachers, hold
the best pews, ride when they are tired, eat when
they are hungry, marry whom they choose, while
I — poor wight!

"Miss Manton." A gentle tap on my door. On
opening it, Rose handed me a card, bearing the
name of Sir Henry Stuart Vernon!

I shall not tell you where I hid it, dear Diary; but I assure you it was in the safest imaginable place, and one which it would puzzle a lawyer to find.

By the time I reached the foot of the staircase, kings, queens, great men and women, had all vanished into thin air.

As I entered our wee parlor, Sir Henry rose to meet me.

After exchanging the usual salutations, he informed me that his friend Arthur had gone to call on Miss Maverick, and invited him to accompany him; but he plead a previous engagement.

We talked over our trip of the previous day, — the beautiful scenery on the Hudson, Judge Francis and his family.

"I am greatly surprised to learn that Judge Blake is your grandfather; and, now that I have been made acquainted with the fact, I see how much you resemble him. Does he remain long in England?" Sir Henry inquired.

"A few months only," I replied. "I hope to have the pleasure of visiting Europe before his return."

"If I should be in England during your visit, Miss Manton, it would give me great pleasure to welcome you to Helm Lodge," said Sir Henry.

I thanked him, but it was all I could say. To tell the truth, — I may as well confess my miserable secret at once, — my whole heart is his! Yes, if you can credit it, given without asking! Is not my state truly deplorable? And he — plighted to another!

I wish I could fly away from myself and every other body, for I blush at my own weakness. It is of no use; help it I cannot. I have tried my utmost to conquer my love, by calling my pride, my principle, to my aid; but I may as well call upon the waters. I have fully proved that *nothing* will quench my deep, pure love for Sir Henry!

What a record against myself! Poor, unworthy me! What *would* grandpa say, should *he* divine my secret?

I fear it would be a long day before he would invite me to visit him!

Sir Henry asked me to favor him with a song. Of course I replied, "Certainly, if you wish;" and, rising, he accompanied me to the piano.

After singing several plaintive songs, and one or

two duets, pa and ma entered. After the usual form of introduction, — I cannot tell how, — the subject of "Woman's Rights," the principal topic of the day, was introduced.

I kept myself a little in the background, as much so as modesty would suggest, leaving pa and ma to engross the conversation, save when Sir Henry turned upon me an inquiring look.

Pa asked Sir Henry's opinion.

"To tell you the plain truth, sir," Mr. Vernon replied, "I think the great question of the present day should be *men's* rights or wrongs, whichever you may be pleased to call them. These are lost sight of. You hear of nothing, at the present time, but the clamor of women for *their* rights, social and political; but if woman wishes to *be* woman, if she wishes to fill the place for which God has designed her, — that of a loving wife and mother, — let her forever flee the polls!

"If there is any one revolting thought, anything that would make man turn from woman with loathing, it is when he shall see her standing around the corners of the streets, surrounded by a group of men, anxious to buy her vote; bantering, ridiculing her, offering every species of indignity. And who has she to thank but herself? Spanish and Irish, German and French, Yankees and Creoles, — black and white, all in one grand conglomeration! They gave proof of their ability to govern by their dignified behavior at their convention yesterday! Ah, don't mention it, sir; don't mention it."

"How is it, then," said my father, pleasantly, "that you allow a woman at the head of your great nation?"

"Wrong, altogether wrong!" said Sir Henry; — "a remnant of the dark ages. Not that I would say aught against our beloved Queen, for she is a *true* woman, in every sense of the word. I don't know that *she* has an enemy in the world; but still it is my honest conviction that woman is out of the place for which God designed her, when she has, not only a voice, but the reins of government in her hand.

"And what would queens achieve were not man her prime minister, and the controlling agent of her government?

"Throughout the Bible man is spoken of, nay, constituted, the *head* of woman.

" This is one of the most bitter truths that the poor human nature in woman is willing to admit; for I really believe that nine women out of ten think themselves a little superior to the men in everything!"

" Oh, Mr. Vernon, how *can* you?" said I.

" Ah! Miss Manton, you and your honored mother belong to the class that remain over the nine!" said Sir Henry; at which remark we all joined in a hearty laugh.

" What do you think, Mr. Vernon," said pa, " of the remark made by one of our famous lady writers" (we had learned that Gail was the *nom de plume* of a lady!), " ' Wherever man pays reverence to woman, — wherever any man feels the influence of woman purifying, chastening, abashing, strengthening him against temptation, shielding him from evil, ministering to his self-respect, medicining his weariness, peopling his solitude, winning him from sordid prizes, enlivening his monotonous days with mirth, or fancy, or wit, flashing heaven upon his earth, and mellowing it all for spiritual fertility, — there is the element of marriage.'"

" Well sir! first let me ask if the writer of this sentence was *ever* married? and, secondly, taking it for granted that she has been, whether her husband can endorse these sentiments from his own experience?"

"This I cannot answer, sir," pa replied, "but I should like to ask you if you can point me to a single passage in Holy Writ where man is commanded, or even permitted, to *reverence* woman?"

"No sir," said Mr. Vernon.

"If I read my Bible correctly, it makes it incumbent on *the wife* to see that *she reverence her husband!* She must learn in silence, *with all subjection.* She is not suffered to teach or usurp authority over the man, but to be in silence! She is to submit herself unto her husband as unto the Lord! For the husband is *the head* of the wife, even as Christ is the head of the Church.

"Now sir, I am free to confess that it is a hard truth for poor weak woman to consider her husband, if she loves him ever so well, as her liege *lord*, and I doubt not her whole being revolts at it; but my own private opinion is, that it *is a part of the punishment entailed on all the children of Eve!*

"But it is written in unmistakable characters, and it cannot be blotted out, 'Man is a superior being to woman;' and whoso reads his Bible, and receives it as God's Word, must not only *receive* the unwelcome truth, but must live according to it!"

"But, sir," said ma, — who had been silent till this moment, — "but, sir, you must remember that husbands have *their* duties!"

"Very true, very true, my love," said pa; "we will discuss the duties of husbands at some other time.

"We men make no pretensions.

"We know and feel that we are poor, weak, conceited mortals, as much so, every whit, as woman; but the point we are now discussing is 'Woman's *Rights*.' We have yet to learn whether it belongs to her to take up politics as a study! In my own judgment, no one should be allowed the privilege of the polls unless they are educated enough to understand the principles of each party represented.

"Simply being able to read and write is no evidence at all of fitness.

"Scarcely a child of twelve years of age but can read and write as well as most persons at twenty, — but this would not prove a child was fit to vote!

"If I am to be governed, I desire a ruler who is worthy of my respect, — one who will show that he has the good of the nation at heart. He must be a man of sound sense and discrimination.

"How many of those who vote at the present day know of, or care for, such fitness?"

"Ninety-nine out of one hundred," said pa, "vote because it is their ticket, or their friends' ticket; or, again, they expect to receive a good office, — this latter I think the ruling motive. Some sell their vote for a large price; but when woman comes to the rescue, where, oh where, will our country be?"

"Why is it, then," said Sir Henry, "that the feeling seems to be widening and deepening in favor of this subject?"

"I cannot answer, sir; save that if woman undertakes a thing, such is her indomitable perseverance, she generally carries the day!

"There may be another reason, also," said pa. "Take the large majority of women, and while their husbands are absent in the evening, attending lectures, — sitting in some reading-room, or bar-room, perchance, or snugly ensconced at the theatre, — the poor wife, who never knows when her work is done, is at home, tending the baby, mending the clothes; in fact, doing anything but enjoying a leisure hour in reading.

"If she finds time to read a few verses in her Bible before she retires, it is all that she can do."

"Ah!" replied ma, "you have hit the true reason, dear. I think myself this is the why and wherefore so many in our land are rising to assert what they consider their rights. I have heard some of these women defending their position on the plea that they knew no variety in life, — no change of any kind, — but the same humdrum existence the year in and the year out!

"The large majority not only have the care of their house, — cooking, washing, ironing, making and mending, but the care of their infant children beside, — which latter care the poor husbands would think enough in itself to kill any man of moderate strength!

"In many cases these husbands will come home at night without a word of sympathy or kindness; and, instead of bringing some interesting book from the library, and reading to the poor wife as she plies the needle with her weary fingers for him and his, he will leave his tea-table as soon as he has satisfied his demands, having taken every choice bit that was before him, utterly regardless of her whom he has promised to love as his own body, whether she has much or little herself to eat; and, instead of amusing his little ones, — which it is as much his duty to do as her own, — and relieving her weary frame for an hour, perhaps, he takes his hat, often with the only remark, 'I must be out of this!' and leaves her solitary and alone."

" But," said Mr. Vernon, " must not women blame themselves, to some extent, for the indifferent treatment which they often receive from their husbands? During the first few months of married life they are very careful to be dressed in the most becoming style, — to arrange their hair with the greatest care, — to be decked with collars and cuffs of snowy whiteness. They are not only punctual at breakfast, but are very careful that their husband's taste shall be gratified in every article of diet; in a word, they treat him as if they loved him *better* than themselves.

"Now, in my opinion, if women continued to show this lovingkindness, they would seldom find occasion to complain of indifference on the part of men; for any man with a soul would appreciate such a wife.

"After the first six months of married life, the majority of women will go down to breakfast with their hair in papers or braids, — a soiled collar, — slatternly in their whole appearance.

"In a short time they find it impossible to rise so early; and, if their husband must go to his business at such an unseasonable hour, they think it quite as well for him to breakfast alone; and so on, from step to step, till the poor husband finds that his fond anticipations of happiness were but an idle dream; consequently he determines to become indifferent, and evince no pleasure in one so utterly unworthy to bear the name of wife. This is a sad but true picture of many a wedded pair. And poor man must bear the blame. The world cannot look behind the curtain, and see the why and wherefore, — so, of course, the husband is denounced as an unfeeling, horrid creature! Woman carries on the deception by shaking her head in a knowing manner, and saying to every young lady who is thinking of matrimony, 'If you only knew when you were well off, you would trust no man!' And thus man is driven from the little spot which would be the *dearest spot on earth to him*, if his wife would make it ' *Home, sweet Home.'* "

"I agree with you, sir," replied ma, "that there are many such cases to be deplored; still, I think that woman's nature, as a whole, is to be kind to those who show love and sympathy to her. I speak of the middle and lower walks of life; for, I am sorry to say, there is but little of love, or even *true* friendship, among the higher classes.

"As I before said, sir, nine out of ten who favor 'Woman's Rights,' do it to make a change in their daily course. They feel that they shall then be treated with more deference and respect, even though it may be feigned! Their husbands will be obliged to dress them handsomely, to save themselves from sarcastic remark!

"The poor women know also that they must attend the political meetings; and if their spouse pretend to question the necessity, they will, no doubt, assure him that they are now *his equal*, and he may take his turn in staying at home to mind the children, — for it is very important that she should be enlightened on politics, that she may know *how* to vote. She must judge for *herself!* For you know, Mr. Vernon, that all women do not agree with their husbands in politics."

"True, madam, but I trust they are few! for a difference on this point often engenders bitter feelings which not even time will eradicate. My opinion is, from what I have seen since my sojourn in America, that when the women go to the polls they will rule, — and you will have seen the last *Republican* President. There is not a doubt that the Democrats will carry all before them.

"Of course I am not prepared to say that their rule would not be as salutary for the country as that of the Republicans!

"I must say, however, that, next to religion, I should desire my wife to be with me in politics!"

How I wanted to ask him if the Lady Alice Irving was a woman who would be willing to yield her own cherished opinions to those of her husband; but I dare not trust myself to speak her name. I could see that ma was a little uneasy; for, though a more devoted pair never lived than pa and ma, yet they were far apart in politics. Ma, however, adroitly changed the theme, by speaking of the sentiment already advanced, — man's *reverencing* woman!

"I believe," said Sir Henry, "that man not only does, but always will entertain the highest respect for woman, whether he admit it or not, as long as she is worthy of it; but *reverence* is altogether different from respect.

"We apply the term reverence to beings of a superior nature. God says that *man* is such."

I thought, though I dare not utter my thought, that I wish I could receive this truth with the ready acquiescence with which all God's commands *should* be received; but I must confess I, am a trifle rebellious on this point.

The very idea of some of the miserable fops of the present age having a superior nature to ours!

But Sir Henry was talking of *men*, not *fops!* — *their* nature is fallen and degraded! ..

I must own that I am willing to concede that Sir Henry is *my* superior, as also a few others of my acquaintance; but these men are very few.

If man really came up to the Gospel standard, I don't think my heart would rebel as it does.

"But," said Sir Henry, "I am free to admit that the men of to-day are not the men of Bible days.

"The present race of men have fallen, as the angels did, from their first estate. Much of their nature's degradation is owing to accursed pride. And has not woman presented him with this apple also? A proud *man* is an anomaly! Such of them as are really deserving the appellation, are ever found to have a weak spot in their brain. By nature, man is too *noble* to be proud!

"It is his association with *woman* that has made him what he is in this respect.

"You ladies," said Sir Henry, "will excuse my plainness; for I am speaking now of men and women as a class.

"Since the deterioration of the race, woman, the moment she becomes acquired of an increase in this world's goods, begins to feel her importance, and the weaker her intellect the more glaring her folly.

"Does she become the possessor of *ten* thousand, she feels, from that moment, that she is superior to her friend who has only five thousand; when she arrives at *twenty*, she looks down upon her who

has arrived only to ten thousand, and so on: unless
the one with five or ten, perchance, belong to some
old aristocratic family, or have some near relative
who is a professional gentleman, and to whom, could
they but share his title, they would be willing to
yield the whole of their patrimony! — preferring
vastly to be Mrs., — the lawyer or the doctor's wife,
— than poor Miss, with no one to whom they can
bequeath their twenty thousand.

"These poor deluded women rear families, bringing them up with false notions of what constitutes
true greatness.

"These boys and girls become men and women,
again instilling their feelings into the minds of *their*
children; and though men, as they grow older, and
go out into the world, if they have an otherwise
well-balanced mind, rise above these foolish notions,
yet with women they are inherent, and seem to be
a part of their being.

"Take, for instance, the members of one family, —
which, in England, is frequently seen, and I doubt
not may be found as often on America's shore.

"A father, with a moderate fortune, procures a
fine business situation for his sons. They go on for

a while, prospering in their business; marry, have a family around them, and are on the most intimate terms with one another.

" Suddenly one of the brothers die, leaving a moderate fortune for his wife and little ones. They must retrench their expenses; move into a smaller house, and commence the trying life of economy. The other brothers go on amassing wealth.

" They soon remove into larger and more expensive quarters.

" Their children must now make their *entrèe* into society. Everything must be in style to correspond with their father's position in the mercantile community.

" Now comes up the dreaded question, ' Shall we invite our nieces to the party?'

" ' Certainly,' replied the father. ' Why do you ask such a question?'

" ' Because,' replies the wife, ' I think they would be out of place.'

" ' They are known to be in depressed circumstances, and have no garments in which it would be suitable to appear.'

" ' I don't know about this,' answered the husband.

'They are as highly educated in every respect as our own children, and would appear quite as well.

"'They need not be over-dressed, but modestly, and yet well enough not to attract attention. Perhaps, by our notice, they will continue to receive attention on our account, and may thus secure some desirable partner for life.'

"'It is no use for you to talk thus,' replied the loving wife. 'Anything but being obliged to have one's poor relations ever hanging around; it will only instil envy into their hearts, and numerous other sins beside. Then, Mr. S. and Mr. L. will be here, and what will they think, to meet persons so humbly situated in life?' Could she have looked for a moment into the heart of Mr. S., whom she was endeavoring to secure for her own daughter, she would have found herself greatly mistaken in the motives that would actuate him in the choice of a wife!

"And thus this wife and mother gains the ascendancy over her husband, quiets his conscience, and he goes away to his counting-room.

"A month or two after the papers herald a donation from Mr. ——, of fifty thousand, to Oxford, —

the world read in astonishment, — and bitter are the remarks made at his expense!

" ' Better have given it to his brother's widow! Would you believe it? He gave a large party a few weeks since, and slighted his own relations because they were not wealthy!'

"And yet this poor man," said Sir Henry, "was more sinned against than sinning!

"If the woman whom God gave him to be a helpmeet had *encouraged* rather than tempted him; using her influence, — 'strengthening him against temptation,' if he had have been weak enough to be thus tempted, — had she, with the instinct of a *true* woman, as God made her to be, plead the cause of those poor afflicted ones, and have said to her husband, ' Instead of giving fifty thousand to Oxford, settle the amount on your brother's widow and orphans, and let it be known that when the girls are married you will give them a dowry, for they are fitted to grace any circle!

" ' Remember, my dear husband, the old adage, " Charity begins at home!" and though your name may not be enrolled among the munificent donors to our seminaries, yet, when your last hour shall come, it will be found entered on that great book where the angel records the *good* as well as the evil deeds,' how different the result!

" Any woman who would act thus, I should think worthy to receive the *highest* place in the esteem of man.

" I am sorry to say," continued Sir Henry, " that women do not often show such phases of character. In this respect she merits anything but the *reverence* of her husband!

" Christian women, too, have reason to mourn day after day for indulging in pride. Many of them, though, have so benumbed their conscience as to consider it a virtue rather than a vice!

" Until woman is divested of this weak, crying sin of the age, she is not *worthy* the reverence of man.

" Once let *man* take an independent stand, and say he *despises* any woman who is puffed up with her own importance, and there would very soon be a new era among us!

" The idea of *woman's shielding man from evil!*

" I have no patience with such sentiments," said Sir Henry.

" This writer, whoever she may be, is laboring against the mighty truths of Scripture, and reversing the order of things. She is not content with holding up woman as she *is*, but she will not rest until she makes her the *head* of man !

" I always considered it the privilege of the greater to shield the weaker.

" I am willing to admit, however, that woman, under some circumstances, has it in her power, *at times*, to shield men from evil !

" The husband, if he is worthy the *name* of husband, should shield his *wife* from every evil ; and, if she is like the woman that King Lemuel describes, he will delight to do it !

" My theory is," said Sir Henry, " that when two are united in that perfect love of which the *Bible* speaks, — each filling their own sphere, as designated by the words of Holy Writ, — then you have the true element of marriage. If we are permitted to live in the Millennium, we shall then see men and women in their true characters !

" They will then be just as God made and designed them to be, — ' *in honor preferring one another!*' "

We all agreed with Sir Henry, that we hoped we may live to see that happy·time.

The evening was now far advanced, and Sir Henry rose to leave, not without receiving a cordial invitation to visit us as often as his many engagements would allow.

He said he should pass the remainder of the month only in New York, as he must then leave for the far West.

How my heart sank with these words!

X.

UNCLE FRANCIS came in this morning, and handed me a letter from grandpa.

It was the looked-for invitation to visit him in Europe. I had no idea of receiving it before the fall; but there were reasons why grandpa thought it best for me to go earlier. And so I am going abroad!

What an amount of knowledge you will glean, you dear little Diary, for I am determined to place everything worthy of note in your keeping!

My kind grandpa enclosed in the letter a check for five hundred, with which to purchase my ticket and an outfit.

I suppose the poor white muslin will have to figure, if I receive any attention. But stay, — per-

haps pa may not object to my carrying the fine
clothes that I wore in Milledgeville, and then I
may be able to save money enough to buy a new
suit for Frank, who enters college this fall.

Pa is anxious Frank should enter *Yale*, as he pur-
sued his studies there ; but I think he will be obliged
to yield his preference to uncle Francis, as he is to
defray his expenses, and permit him to enter Harvard, uncle Francis's Alma Mater !

And now I must recall my wandering thoughts,
and try to learn something of the great country which
I am so soon to visit. I have learned a little about
its present Sovereigns, and I remember some of its
prominent characters, who live only in history ; but
I fear, if I should be questioned as to my actual
knowledge, I should do but little credit to myself
or my teachers. And whom shall I select as my
first study ?

There are Pope and Dryden, Shakespeare and
Bacon, Byron and Thompson, Cowper and Milton,
beside Wordsworth, Goldsmith, Young, Gray, Campbell, Beattie, Watts, Johnson, Sheridan and Burke ;
not forgetting my loved Bunyan, Hemans, Howitt,
Tennyson, and Crowley, Dickens and Hogarth, —

his father-in-law, — Thackeray and Bronte, Scott, and my much-admired Burns!

Next in order, as of course I give the preference to English and Scottish characters first, come Fenelon, Le Sage, Rousseau, Buffon, Chateaubriand, Hugo, De Vigny, Thiers, De Tocqueville, and Dudevant, of France. Luther, Zwinglii, Melancthon, Albrecht Durer, Von Humboldt, Grimm, Goethe, Schiller, Voss, and Schelling, of Germany. Homer, Hesiod, Sophocles, Plutarch, Strabo, and Valaorites, of Greece, — who are but the very beginning of the list.

Then come the musical celebrities, painters, curiosities. Dear me! I may as well give up in despair, for if I once commence there will be no end!

And before I begin studying about other lands, I think I should know more of my own. There are Webster and Choate, Clay and Everett. I suppose ma would say Bell and Johnson, and pa would add Chase and Lincoln, and Frank would add *Sumner*, for Frank is about as great a radical as well can be! Uncle Francis has instilled his ideas into him; and this is the way with these Northerners, — they have such narrow, contracted views!

Were I called upon, I should add to the list
Evarts. He is *my* beau ideal of true greatness.
Any man who has the moral courage to stand up
for the right among us, in these days, is a *great*
man!

Ma insists upon it that it is *mob* rule, when the
majority carry a point which they know is actually
forbidden by law, under the plea of reconstruction,
and such like! But I've no time for discussing the
right or wrong of the matter; suffice it to say, that
if President Grant restores our country to its former
prosperity, and if in four years women are allowed
to vote, I will promise him *my* vote for his re-
election!

Among the musical celebrities with whose history
I must become acquainted are Handel, Haydn,
Mozart, Bach, Beethoven, Lizt, Mendelssohn, Schu-
bert, Moschelles and Wagner: Chopin and Bennett
I am familiar with; and also the famous songstresses,
Lind, Piccolomini, Alboni, Sontag, Malibran, Paton,
Catalani, Parepa, with Phillips and Kellogg of our
own land.

It is a true remark that the more a man knows, the
more he feels he has to learn. If I study hard for two

years, I shall but have just begun. But I *will* not be discouraged! I will devote an hour, at least, a day to improving my mind, even if I take it from my sleeping hours; for I should never survive the mortification of being classed by the eminent literary characters among whom I shall be thrown as a young lady of *uncultivated* mind.

And it is my own fault that I am thus ignorant! I confess with shame that I am too fond of that class of reading which requires no thought, rather than that of a more solid nature.

Pa says that if one is determined to indulge only in a high class of literature, the more will he thirst for it, and turn with contempt from the idle trash which finds such multidudes of readers.

As the mind is cultivated, it will expand and grow in the desire for that which tends only to edification. I believe I see myself in a new light!

From this moment I resolve I will no longer indulge in sentimental reading, or allow my mind to be overrun with weeds and brambles, but will strive to grow daily in the knowledge of God and man.

And now let me see with whom I shall commence, — I think I will take Shakespeare:

William Shakespeare was born in Stratford-upon-Avon, Warwickshire, in 1564.

His father was John Shakespeare, a well-to-do farmer of Snitterfield, about three miles from Stratford.

His mother was Mary Arden, the youngest daughter of Robert Arden of Wilmecote, who were of the acknowledged gentry of Warwickshire — their family being ancient, and of some note in the county. William was the first son of a family of eight. Nothing certain is known of his life and education in his younger days, save that he attended a free grammar-school at Stratford.

He knew enough of Latin to understand such passages as he met in the course of his reading, as also a little Italian and French. He married Anne Hathaway, a daughter of Richard Hathaway, a yeoman of Shottery.

This young woman was eight years older than Shakespeare. At the time he was married he was eighteen, and she twenty-six. His wife was said to be beautiful.

He was the father of three children, one of whom married a physician, Dr. John Hall. It is uncertain which was the first production of Shakespeare, but he is said to have written thirty-seven plays. With the nobles, wits, and poets of the day, he was in friendly intercourse. He had some knowledge of law, of which his plays afford good evidence.

In 1586 he visited London, where he performed in some of his own plays; for he was not only a celebrated *author*, but *actor*.

His first published poem, Venus and Adonis, he dedicated to the Earl of Southampton, an accomplished nobleman, who loved literature and encouraged men of letters.

The second part of Henry Fourth portrays the supremacy of his powers as poet, dramatist, philosopher, wit and humorist combined. Falstaff, Merry Wives of Windsor, Hamlet, Taming the Shrew, and Midsummer Night's Dream, were received with much favor.

It is probable that Titus Adronicus is the earliest dramatic effort of his pen. He was a little more than twenty-three years of age when it was composed.

He appears very early in his career to have attained a share in the direction and emoluments of the theatre to which he was attached. Besides the composition of his own plays, he often revised and remodelled the works of others.

Pecuniary emolument and literary reputation were not the only reward that our hero received. Queen Elizabeth gave him many marks of her favor; and so delighted was she with Falstaff, that she desired him to continue him in another play, and exhibit him in love; — when followed the Merry Wives of Windsor. James the First also wrote him a letter, with his own hand.

Dr. Ben Jonson, a literary character of high repute, was a great friend of Shakespeare.

Shakespeare was godfather to one of his children; and, after the christening, being in deep study, Jonson came to cheer him up, and asked him why he was so melancholy?

"I have been considering a great while," said Shakespeare, "what should be the fittest gift for me to bestow upon my godchild, and I have resolved at last!"

"Prithee, what?" said he.

"I'faith, Ben, I'll e'en give her a dozen good Latin (latteen-brass) spoons, and thou shalt *translate* them."

"The above," says Archdeacon Nares, "is a pleasant raillery on Jonson's love for translating."

The cause of Shakespeare's death is unknown. He died in 1616, in his fifty-second year, and was buried on the north side of the chancel of the great church of Stratford.

Here a monument, containing a bust of the poet, was erected to his memory. A cenotaph has since been erected to his memory in Westminster Abbey.

He was contemporaneous with Cervantes, who, a little singularly, died on the same day. And who was Cervantes? All I know is, that he was a Spaniard. I have found, on examination, that —

Cervantes, the author of "Don Quixote," was the son of Rodrigo, descended from an ancient Gallician family, and his mother, Leonara de Cortinas, was a lady of refinement. He was born in Spain, in 1547.

He was of fair complexion, his eyes blue, his hair auburn. He was of handsome, spirited countenance, cheerful in his manners, and beloved in every relation of life.

In 1584, he married an accomplished lady of Esquirias.

The death of Philip Second, in 1598, brought an end to the despotic rule in Spain, which was felt in the world of letters.

Cervantes could not give free vent to his opinions. Mankind began to grow tired of the hypocrisy, sentimentality, and folly of the books of chivalry. Old Spain longed for some free-spoken word which would end the weary spectacle of an effete literature, and Cervantes uttered that word.

It was "Don Quixote!" As for his miscellaneous literary productions, they are almost forgotten in the triumph achieved by Don Quixote. Yet this great man was buried, without any kind of distinction, in the convent of the nuns of Trinity, Catle del Humilladero, and nothing but a common tombstone marks the place where his ashes were removed at a subsequent period. In 1835 a bronze statue of him, larger than life, was placed in the Plaza del Estamento, at Madrid, and a small bust was placed, in 1834, by one of his admirers, over the door of the house in which he died.

Next in order I think I will select some one of

the musical celebrities of the day, and learn something of his history; and as Mendelssohn is one of my favorites, he shall be my choice.

Felix Mendelssohn Bartholdy was born in Hamburg, in 1809. His father was connected with one of the first banking-houses in Europe. Goethe was foremost among the distinguished persons who became interested in his precocious genius.

He was not six years old when he performed, with skill, upon the piano; in fact, he could sing almost before he could speak. Being advised by competent judges, his father determined that he should make music a profession. Zelter, the friend of Goethe, was his instructor in composition, and Berger his teacher on the piano.

When only nine years old he gave his first public concert in Berlin, and a year later he appeared before the public in Paris. From this time he commenced to write compositions for the piano, violin, and violincello. He seemed to be raised to fill the gap caused by the death of Beethoven.

His Midsummer Night's Dream, his music for Goethe's Walpurgis night, the Dediphus of Sophocles, besides a number of admirable sonatas, concerts, etc., are among his works.

But his "Songs without Words" are filled with new beauty, and will ever be regarded as *gems* by every one who is possessed of a soul attuned to such harmonies. His fame, however, rests upon his Oratorios. St. Paul and Elijah are regarded among his crowning works.

Mendelssohn was much beloved for the beauty of his character. As he was permitted to indulge his tastes without hindrance, he was spared the trials which are the lot of all who are aspirants for public fame.

His health was impaired by grief on account of his sister's death; and although he laid by his work and took a tour through Switzerland, it brought only temporary relief, and he died, in the prime of his manhood, from affection of the brain, at Leipsic, in 1847.

Now I must take the time to study a little about Goethe; for if he was Mendelssohn's friend, he must be worth knowing something about.

Johann Wolfgang Von Goethe was the most literary man of the nineteenth century. He was born in

Frankfort-on-the-Main in 1749, and died in Weimar in 1832.

He was very precocious, lively and sensitive. Before he was ten years old he wrote in several languages, invented stories, and meditated poems.

His youth and beauty, his frank manner, and, above all, his genius, made him the delight of every circle. He was constantly falling in love, and as often did he break away from the object of his attachment.

At the age of sixteen he was sent to Leipsic to commence his collegiate studies. Soon after entering upon them he wrote two dramas, not much in themselves, but indicating his dawning powers.

When in Wetzlar, he fell in love with a young lady who was already engaged, and who was soon after married. A young and melancholy student with whom he was intimate, having committed suicide because of a similar passion for the wife of one of his friends, Goethe wove the incidents of the two cases into a novel, which he called the "Sufferings of Young Werther," which was received throughout Europe with the most prodigious sensation. Its chief success, however, arose from the fact that it expressed a sad longing and discontent, which was a striking characteristic of the age.

This was followed by other dramas, when Goethe acquired such fame that he was invited by the Grand Duke of Saxe Weimar to pass a few weeks at his court, where such a friendship sprang up between the prince and the poet, that Goethe from that time made Weimar his permanent residence.

After so many affaires de la cœur he picked a broken twig at last, by marrying Christine Vulpius, who was uneducated, and served in some domestic capacity in his house.

One year after the completion of his celebrated drama of " Faust," he was taken ill of a cold, which terminated in a fever, and which resulted fatally, in the eighty-third year of his age.

MARCH 13th.

Just as I had finished, yesterday, learning something about Goethe, Belle Schuyler called, and told me a piece of news which I can scarcely credit!

She said that she had just left Harry Hamilton, and that he confided to her the engagement between Arthur Jenkins and my own dear Minnie.

Now I cannot believe that I, who am Minnie's bosom friend, should have to learn this, if a fact, from another; and therefore I shall not credit one word until I learn it from Minnie herself.

I think I could not forgive her, if true, for allowing me to hear it first from strangers, — and yet not a stranger exactly, for Belle is one of our intimates, — but I feel a little sore about the matter. Report says that Belle and Harry Hamilton are on the verge of being betrothed, and perhaps this accounts for Harry's confiding in Belle!

Now that I think of it, she did say that Harry *confided* it to her.

Dear me! What geniuses women are! They can neither keep their own secrets nor any one's else; but then, there are exceptions. I would not trust *my* secret, no, not even to Minnie, my bosom friend, for I scarcely dare whisper it to myself; so it will not do to condemn *all* for the foible of the many!

While Belle was sitting with me, Chloe handed me a note, which, as I glanced at, I knew to be from Minnie; but I put it in my pocket to read after Belle had taken her departure.

I joked Belle a little about Harry, when she laughingly replied, "People that live in glass houses should not throw stones!" When I asked her to explain herself, she replied that "people are not blind in these days!"

"Don't you think, Kate, that people see not only the deference, but the preference with which Sir Henry ever treats you?"

At these words, I blushed the deepest scarlet; but, trying to assume a careless demeanor, I replied, "People do not always look through the right glass. Sir Henry Vernon is already betrothed to the Lady Alice Irving!"

"Kate Manton! tell me: do *you* believe that idle tale? Harry says it is a report which Arthur Jenkins, knowing how very exalted Sir Henry's ideas were of what a woman should be, circulated, to prevent the girls from making fools of themselves; and you may depend upon it, that, if Minnie and Arthur *are* engaged, you will find the truth of my assertion before many days."

I could scarcely compose my voice enough to answer, "Belle, you know that Sir Henry Vernon would never, for a moment, think seriously of me, even were his heart in his own keeping; for you know I am a *poor* girl!

"*Wealth* is nothing with him! Harry says that Arthur told him Sir Henry had money enough, and all that he asked for in a wife were character and heart; some one to love and respect him, — love him for himself alone! If you think, Kate, that people do not see the admiring glances that he casts on you, you are greatly mistaken. I have caught him myself looking at you, and then have seen him start as if he were a culprit. The day we visited West Point, when on board the boat, I saw him, as you were walking away, after having introduced him to Judge Francis, turn and look at you, and then turn to the Judge and make a remark, and for five minutes they were in earnest conversation; and I am perfectly sure, Kate, it was about *you.* So cheer up, Katie dear. Though one thing more: if you are so fortunate as to win him, I trust you will set the example to the world not to discard your friends who have been less fortunate than yourself; though, if I must tell the truth, I wouldn't exchange Harry for twenty of Sir Henry!"

"Ah, Belle," said I, "now you must own to the

fair impeachment, that you are really engaged to
Harry!"

"Yes, Kate," she replied, "I am only too happy
to reply in the affirmative, and will tell you that it
is just a week to-day since I promised to be his
wife.   Harry says it may be five years before he
is able to wed, it costs so much to support a wife
at the present day.   I told him that, notwithstanding
he was such a horrid creature as to make such an
assertion, I should rather wait ten years for him
than wed another; and that, though it did cost a
fortune to live even decently in this age, yet I did
not doubt his own expenses would be lessened by
one-half, when he had *me* to take care of him!"

"Were young ladies what they should be," replied I, "the young men would not be so timid
about marrying.

"In the good old days of yore, if a couple were
married, and had but part of a house to occupy,
they thought themselves well off!   They made no
pretensions to greatness; they were willing to begin
life as their fathers did before them, and live pru-
dently and quietly, for themselves, their families, and

their God; and their basket and store was blessed, and they rose to eminence, slowly but surely.

"But in these days our young men and women are not willing to plod along step by step; they wish to begin where their fathers left off!

"If there is to be any plodding, it must be *before* marriage; for it would be very difficult in these days to find a young lady who would be willing to accommodate herself to a *small* income; and here is one of '*men's wrongs.*'

"The young man, instead of finding the one who has promised to love and live for him alone, willing to wear a single rather than a double skirt, could she but be rewarded for her self-denial by sharing his home, his cares, his labors, — instead of being cheered and encouraged by her loving words and presence, as he returns to his home night after night, finds that he must work *alone*, day after day, year after year, till, when the time shall arrive that he is able to wed his betrothed, she will have verged toward that unhappy period when she will be *obliged* to wear double skirts, Grecian bend, chignons, and all other kinds of nonsensical superfluities, to save herself from the appellation of 'old maid.'

"It is all wrong, *all* wrong! And *who* is to be blamed?

"The women place the grave charge upon the shoulders of the men, and say that a young gentleman will take no notice of a young lady unless she is dressed in these fashionable appendages, and that any young girl, though she may not be upward of twenty, should she dare dress plainer than the acknowledged style, would be denounced as a '*regular* old maid'; consequently every nerve is strained, and all kinds of self-denial practised by the parents, to dress the female portion of their family in an attractive manner!

"And thus *dress* is about the only subject that fills the minds of our young ladies. 'How do I look? Will he think my dress becoming? Am I stylish-looking?'

"Vain butterflies! how well fitted to take the care of a man's household, — to train up his children, if he is *blessed* (?) with any! Oh no! they could not *think* of taking care of their own babe! it is *exceedingly* vulgar to take charge of your own infant. 'My dear,' says the young wife, 'you must hire a nursery-girl at once!' There are two hun-

dred dollars more a year, to say nothing of light
fingers and board; and while the poor father bends
before this blast, he says, 'I suppose it must be all
right!' Who blames the young men for shrinking
from marriage? I do not, for one!"

"Nor I either," replied Belle, — "and I really
believe it is one reason why so many young men are
fast! for those among them who have a salary from
which they can put by anything for the future, are
the exception.

"The large majority have salaries that will support *themselves* handsomely — but with a wife only
respectably; and there are few young ladies to be
found that love a man well enough to marry him,
unless they can appear as well as their neighbors."

"The truth is, Belle," said I, "our young people
lack *real, genuine independence!*

"They want the power to say, 'I cannot *afford*
this; I *prefer* — the world to the contrary — to take
the charge of my own little one, whom God has
intrusted to *my* care, rather than delegate it to
another!'

"We need *entire* reformation!

"If women would only think more of their souls

than their frail bodies, — if they would study how to accomplish the most good during the few years of their sojourn in this world of sin and sorrow, — if some among them would introduce reform, and set an example by dressing plainly, by frowning on the many unnecessary appendages to the toilet, even if they do cost but a quarter here and a half there, and which in a short time run away with a sum, though the leak is so small as to be invisible, — that would save them from want in the future.

"What beauty is there in yards of velvet ribbon hanging over their shoulders? in making dresses in such a style as to require yards of fringe to decorate it?

"This aping our superiors in wealth is *small* business. It is one of Satan's devices to steal women's souls. It not only fosters pride, but leads to dishonesty, selfishness, and hypocrisy.

"If there is any woman worthy of being the wife of the most honored man in the community, e'en though she may be poor in purse, yet if she is rich in accomplishments, in a well-balanced and cultivated mind, it is she who is not afraid to say, ' I *cannot afford* many things which I should like, if practicable, but I strive to be content with such as God has been pleased to give me.' Any woman who in this age is not afraid to say she has *no* expectations, is a prize!"

"Well," said Belle, who had been listening with an interested but amused expression during this harangue, "well, Kate, I suppose, then, *you* must be that prize!"

"Ah, Belle," said I, "you surely cannot be so cruel as to say, or even think, I for a moment thought of myself!

"I am a poor, weak, erring mortal, constantly 'doing the things I ought not to do, and leaving undone the things I ought to do, and there is no good in me!' still I confess to you, dear Belle, that our reverses have opened my eyes to a more just view of things than would have been possible had I never have been afflicted.

"The fact is, though I admit man is of a *superior* nature, yet I feel, to a certain extent, that he is susceptible to the influence of woman.

"If finery is the order of the day, he would blush, should he chance meet one of his gay acquaintances, as he was escorting a young lady like myself, clad

in plain clothes, lest they should think she couldn't
be much!

"I feel impressed, more and more, that much of
the sin and folly of the present age is to be laid at
woman's door!

"And who will *immortalize* herself by commencing the work of reform?

"If woman,—no matter how unbounded her
wealth, how enviable and exalted her position,—
if woman only knew the laurels that would crown
her brow, the respect and admiration which she
would elicit from every man whose opinion was anything worth,—not many days would elapse before the
dawning of a brighter, holier day; then will the
teachings of the apostle bring forth fruit, and 'women
will adorn themselves in modest apparel, with shame-
facedness and sobriety, not with broidered hair, or
gold, or pearls, or costly array, but which becometh
women professing godliness and good works.'"

"True," said Belle, "but this latter clause is advice
to women professing godliness, or to *Christians!*"

"Yes, Belle," said I, "but all women should *be*
Christians!

"I don't believe you would find a man living who

would not think higher of woman if she thought more of her mind and less of her body."

"Then they should practise themselves what they preach," said Belle; "I don't think *they* need say anything, for they are just as proud of their imperials and mustaches as the ladies of their chignons! The bare idea of their taking time to *wax* the ends of their mustaches! I'm sure I wouldn't kiss one of these deluded mortals if I *never* kissed a gentleman!"

"I agree with you, Belle," said I, "that the men *are* weak, in adorning their persons to such an extent; still, I think if the ladies would lead by example, and not bestow a smile on a fop or a dandy, you would soon perceive a change in man also."

"Well, I for one, Kate," said Belle, "will advocate no such doctrine. If man is the *superior*, *noble being* that he proves by Scripture he is, *then let him set the example to poor, weak, dependent woman!*

"If *he* should inaugurate the change, we should commence a new era before the close of 1869."

"You may err in some measure, dear Belle, as

11

may I. I do not pretend to infallibility; but there
is a grievous wrong somewhere, and we see its effects
on the rising generation. The last generation, as
a whole, were fast, the present faster, and I fear
the next will be fastest!"

After Belle left I opened Minnie's note, and found
it to contain the pleasing information that she and
Arthur were engaged, and that I was the first one
to whom she had confided the secret; so Arthur
must have told Harry Hamilton!

Minnie is a darling girl; and if Arthur is as true
in performing his duties as a husband, as she will
be as a wife, it will be a happy union indeed!

XI.

MARCH 17th.

LAST evening Minnie and Arthur came over to call. Minnie handed me a small envelope, containing an invitation, which she wished me to answer verbally before her return.

Judge of my astonishment, and of my indescribable sensations of pleasure, when I learned that the next day Mr. Maverick and Minnie were going on to Niagara to engage their rooms for the summer; and, as Mrs. Maverick did not care particularly about leaving home, and Minnie didn't wish to go alone, Mrs. Maverick, in her delicate way, sent me her ticket, asking me to fill her place to Minnie as well as I could!

It is just like her. I knew she did it to give me pleasure, and in such a delicate way, too,—as if I was conferring the favor rather than herself.

Of course my toilette was appropriate, as we should pass but one night at the Falls, and it was too early for company at the hotels. My suit is very pretty. It is of Empress cloth ; and, though it cost but a trifle when compared with the dresses worn by many young ladies, it is very quiet and genteel. It is of a light shade of ashes of roses, trimmed with a fold of silk a shade darker, about an eighth of a yard wide around the bottom of the under-skirt, and the over-skirt trimmed with two folds of half the width. My sack has a head to it, trimmed in the same style. My hat was of felt, the same shade, trimmed with velvet, without feather or flower. Minnie said "she had ample room in her valise to take what few articles I should need."

I first obtained the consent of pa and ma ; and, with Chloe's assistance, soon had my necessary articles packed, and put into the carriage which was at the door.

When I went back to the parlor, there sat pa and ma talking as cosily as possible with Minnie and Arthur. I had to smile, when I thought how soon old married people forget about their *lover* days! I really think it did not once enter the head of my good ma how vastly preferable it would have been to Minnie and Arthur could they have enjoyed each other's society alone, for the few minutes of my absence! But I will do ma the justice to say that she evinces a great deal of thought, generally, on such matters.

I presume if the true state of the case were known, she thought she must come in and thank Minnie for her kindness to her darling child.

And now, in about two hours, I am to start for the world-renowned Niagara! So I must say good-by, at least for one week, to all the famous characters with whom I was to become more intimately acquainted.

II P. M.

Yes, you dear old Diary, I really believe I should rather have left one of my gloves at home than you, you afford me such delight.

Sometimes, by looking in your bright face for a moment, when the clouds look dark around me, I find some spot that chases the sadness away, and bids me hope on, hope ever! And yet, I must own it, " Hope deferred maketh my heart sick."

I cannot claim to have ever known the meaning of *perfect* love, for I have never found any love, as yet, without much fear being connected with it.

At nine o'clock this morning the carriage, with Minnie's sweet face peeping out, stopped at the door. After I had kissed ma again and again, — for I had bidden pa and brother Frank good-by in the morning, — I entered the carriage, and we drove to the station. Minnie said her father would await us there, and she should not be surprised to meet Arthur, also, for a parting word!

How I envied her! Not that I cared for a beau or a husband — *by no* means; but I did want some one to *love* me, and whom I could love, — though I cannot be content with a little. I must be another's *all*, or nothing. And I! what is there in me to attract any one? Just nothing at all.

Tolerably good-looking, decently dressed, and but passably educated! Now I do not think there would have been any necessity for the poet to have breathed his words in my ear, —

> "Oh! if some mighty power were gie us,
> To see ourselves as others see us."

For if any one thinks less of me than I do of myself, I had best retire from social life at once!

As we entered the station, I descried Mr. Maverick — and — could my eyes deceive me? No! it *was* Sir Henry!

Why had *he* come?

Even you, my little Diary, can never tell a *tithe* of my feelings, when he informed me he had joined our party!

He had never visited Niagara, and thought he could not embrace a more favorable opportunity; and as Mr. Maverick was there with *his* watchful eye, there was no impropriety in it.

I do believe that Minnie told ma about it, and that they intended to surprise me.

Such a delightful ride as I had! Of course Mr. Maverick had to take a forward seat, to talk about politics and business with some of his friends whom he met on the train; and, as Arthur sat with Minnie, there was no other alternative for poor Kate Manton but to submit to her fate, and ride to Syracuse in the same seat, and close to the side of Sir Henry.

But I am more than cruel to myself to harbor such

feelings; for it only strengthens them, and makes it more impossible to banish them. Oh! if some kind being, who has suffered in a like predicament, will tell me what I *can* do, I shall be filled with gratitude all my life. I have no strength in myself, for his image is ever present with me!

We pass to-night in Syracuse. Minnie is already in bed, and now I must lay by my pen and prepare to retire, and indulge in dreams of Sir Henry!

Will they ever be realized?

If not, I shall have had a passing pleasure while dreaming. No! no! I will *not* listen to the voice of the syren charming never so wisely; but I will try and say from my heart, —

> " Vain world, with all thy cares, begone —
> Let my religious hours alone;"

for if there is *ever* a time when persons should throw aside all worldliness, it is when they lie down to rest! Our times are not our own, and we may wake in very different circumstances from those in which we compose ourselves to sleep; therefore I will take my Bible, read it, and commit myself unto the Lord.

MARCH 19th, half-past 10, P. M.

We rose this morning quite refreshed, and started at seven o'clock for Niagara. We had time only for a bird's-eye view of Syracuse, as we wished to devote all our spare moments in viewing the Falls, and therefore took the early morning train.

Sir Henry again shared my seat. I was a little embarrassed, as I feared every moment he would introduce some subject on which I was profoundly ignorant.

Can you blame me if I *did* wish to appear well in his eyes?

Is there a young gentleman or lady living who does not wish to appear well in the eyes of the one he or she esteems and loves?

Then receive my advice, and no matter what your situation, your trials, your disadvantages, select an hour or a half hour — nay, even a quarter of an hour, and study on some given subject.

You will be surprised to find how much you can educate your mind in three hundred and sixty-five quarters!

The knowledge thus acquired, will be of great profit to you.

Fortunately for me, — I may say *providentially*, — in the course of our conversation, Sir Henry, alluding to my proposed trip, asked me if I had ever read Shakespeare.

I told him that I read it when quite young, but I was familiar with his life, and the names of most of his plays, and was intending to read them again very soon.

"How remarkable," said I, "that Shakespeare and Cervantes should have died on the same day;" and then I felt like a culprit! I thought I was deceiving him, by conveying the impression that I knew more than I really did; so I added, "I was reading about him yesterday!"

We discussed Irving's merits, and our noble Webster. Then he touched on Mary Queen of Scots, whose history I was fortunate enough to have read a year since, — Scott, Dickens, — who, he informed me, married a daughter of Hogarth; and when I avowed my ignorance of this latter gentleman, he informed me that he was a British author and musician, who resided in London, as musical critic and author, and that his writings were received as standard authority on whatever subject they treated.

He also informed me that Hogarth's daughter, who married Charles Dickens, had been separated from her husband a number of years, and that the sole cause of their separation was uncongeniality of temper.

" How," said Sir Henry, " a man enjoying such world-wide renown could humble himself to allow a separation from his wife and family on so insignificant a plea, is utterly surprising to me. While his place in *English literature* will be as secure as that of Sterne, Fielding, or Scott, yet his place in the hearts of his countrymen can never be that which he would otherwise have held."

I replied "that I was wholly unacquainted with the matter in question; still my own impressions were, that as women promised when they were wed to take their husband for *worse* as well as for better, for *poorer* as well as for richer, she voluntarily placed herself in a position from which nothing could release her. If woman would learn to control her own proud heart, — and this she cannot do, save by the grace of God, — instead of the bitter retort, the look of injured innocence, which will sometimes increase rather than assuage the tempest, — if she will only strive to be a humble, *forbearing*, loving woman, may she not be the means, in God's hands, of saving her husband?"

" True, Miss Manton, but I fear such women in this age, where folly and vanity reign supreme, are few; and, though I grieve to say it, the men who could appreciate them, still fewer!"

We arrived at the International about one o'clock, and after arranging our toilette, and refreshing ourselves with a lunch, we started for the Falls.

Arthur and Minnie led the way, while Sir Henry and I followed, Mr. Maverick walking some of the time with one, and then with another, expressing his curiosity to witness the effect which the first view of the mighty cataract would produce upon Sir Henry and me, as with the others it was no new sight.

How great was our astonishment, surprise, admiration, and, I may add, veneration, as the magnificent spectacle burst upon our gaze. One must see for himself to conceive any idea of this wonderful work of God.

Never before did I ever feel my littleness to such an extent!

Never before did I have such conceptions of the mighty power of God.

We stood speechless, till it seemed as if the majestic grandeur of the great cascade would overpower us, when Sir Henry broke the silence by saying, in the words of Tennyson, —

> "I would that my tongue could utter
> The thoughts that arise in me!"

And turning to Mr. Maverick, he asked "if the cause of this mighty waterfall had ever been discovered?"

Mr. Maverick replied "that the Niagara river, which connects Erie and Ontario, flows from the north-eastern extremity of Erie, with a swift current, in a northerly direction, for about two miles; then more gently, with the current growing wider, till it divides itself, passing on each side of Grand Island. About fifteen or sixteen miles from Erie it begins to grow narrow again, and descend with great velocity. This is the commencement of the rapids, which continue for about a mile, the waters rolling in great swells as they rush swiftly among the rocks, and terminate below in the mighty cataract."

"Wonderful, most wonderful!" said Sir Henry; and then inquired "how great the descent was supposed to be?"

"It is said to measure one hundred and sixty-four feet on the American, and one hundred and fifty on the Canada side."

The noise of this great waterfall varies with the condition of the atmosphere and wind. Sometimes it is heard at a short distance only, and then again for a distance of from forty to fifty miles.

I think the *particular* wind must have been blowing, causing its loudest echoes, during our visit to-day. Even now it seems as if I must stop my ears to shut out, if possible, the deafening sound. And then again I like to listen to it, and imagine it as I first looked upon it in all its majesty! To-morrow morn we are to be up with the dawn, and drive over to the Canada side, from which the view is said to be much finer than that from our own shore.

MARCH 22d, 10 P. M.

Here we are comfortably lodged in Schenectady. It was dark when we arrived, so I cannot say much about the place. To-morrow we are to go as far as Saratoga, thence by car to Troy, passing the night there, and home by way of the Hudson.

We visited the Canadian side of the Fall this morning. There seems to be more breadth, and a greater volume of water on this side, rather than on the American. We noticed on one rock, that projected into the stream, a short distance above the great Fall, a round tower entirely surrounded by steps; but, as our guide informed us, there was scarcely anything to repay one for ascending them, and as our time was precious, we did not attempt it.

We crossed, however, on to Goat's Island. This extends to the brink of the cataract, leaving the river, on the American side, about eleven hundred feet wide, and on the Canadian side twice that width. I am surprised at the large amount of fresh-water shells lying around in the beds of gravel and sand.

It seems as though I had enjoyed a life of happiness in these few hours!

I *ought* to be miserable! Before another month

has passed away, Sir Henry and I will be separated,
— *probably* forever!

And I *love* him so!

His voice, his words, are full of sympathy and
interest; but he hasn't given me a glance, — in fact,
I believe he has not raised his eyes to mine since
we started, and I have done expecting it.

And it *is* best.

A continuation of interchange of feeling would
be productive only of misery to both. Misery! because we can never be more to each other than we
now are. In a few months more he will be settled
in his own home, with the Lady Alice; and I?

Alone!

APRIL 4th.

Here I am at last, safely at home, in my own
room, with my dear little Diary! If one has never
kept a diary, permit me to say, Begin from this time,
and keep one. It will more than repay you for the
time you may expend upon it. It not only refreshes
the memory, by bringing back pleasant scenes that
would otherwise pass into oblivion, but it helps us

to remember the many weaknesses and temptations from which we have been delivered.

How much has transpired since my last entry, which was made in Schenectady! We started for Saratoga at six o'clock the next morning.

It was a bright, glorious morning!

Sir Henry declared he was reminded more of Old England than at any time during his visit in America.

We visited the famous Saratoga Springs, where we partook of as much of the water as we could prevail upon ourselves to drink.

As we were looking around, an old man, who appeared to be an Indian, came up to us, and said " he would recommend us to try some of the water from the *High Rock Spring*, as it contained a larger proportion of iron than the Congress or Iodine."

We thought we had drank as much of the water as would suffice for that day, so Mr. Maverick told him " we should certainly take his advice, and try the High Rock at our next visit there."

The gentlemen each gave the poor man a shilling, for which he seemed truly grateful.

12

I learned here that large quantities of the Congress and Empire Springs were bottled and exported.

We had not time to visit the lake, as it was about three miles distant, and we had only an hour before we started for Troy.

We therefore returned to the hotel, lunched, and then proceeded to the depot, where we took the cars for Troy.

All this time I was the companion of Sir Henry, as Arthur and Minnie were completely engrossed with each other.

Was I glad? Indeed I was. I was enjoying the only *real* happiness of my life.

And what a trifle to find happiness in, of such moment! Simply being the companion of a gentleman, who, after a week or two more has passed, will leave me to my own desolate heart.

Well! I can't help it, and I don't want to, either!

I think it much the best way to adopt ma's plan, and live by the day, — taking the blessings of Heaven as they fall in our path!

I feel that I possess vastly more than such an

irritable, uncharitable, censorious spirit should have, but I hope for better things.

I am going to begin a new life. I am determined to live in single blessedness, and devote myself to doing good in every possible way; in a word, I'll forget myself and live for God!

When we arrived in Troy, my attention was drawn by Sir Henry to a fine building built in the Byzantine style, situated on a commanding eminence of Mount Ida, and which Mr. Maverick informed us was the Troy University.

I had thought of Troy as a place of ordinary importance only, and was completely taken by surprise when I beheld its size, heard the noise, and witnessed the appearance of business that everywhere appeared on the streets.

It is laid out with great regularity, though the principal street follows the river, and is somewhat curved.

The streets are mostly about sixty feet wide, well paved, with good sidewalks, and ornamented by trees.

The houses are neat and tasty, and some of the buildings are elegant.

The court-house is built of marble, with a Grecian front of the Doric order.

There was an old house which I had heard of, built in 1752, by Vanderheyden, which we wished to visit, but time forbade.

We took the boat, at three o'clock, for home. Never was there anything more romantic, more enchanting, than that sail down the Hudson.

We were more struck by the quiet grandeur and imposing appearance of the Catskill Mountains than that of any other scenery along the route. Mr. Maverick remarked, that if we could be so fortunate as to view them from the Highlands at the time the sun descended behind their summits and gilded them with his parting rays, we should witness a most beautiful display of colors, which, if depicted upon canvas, would be regarded as an exaggeration of the painter.

Upon one of the terraces of the mountain stands the "Mountain House," at an elevation of two thousand five hundred feet above the river, which is said to be a cool and quiet retreat from the heat and bustle of the city.

As the day closed, the moon arose in all her splendor.

A charming band on board, which I learned from Mr. Maverick was "Dodworth's" celebrated band, was discoursing the sweetest music.

Sir Henry and I promenaded the deck, stopping occasionally to look over the vessel's side and watch her as she glided so peacefully along.

We said but little, though one, I'm sure, was thinking much.

"Next week I leave for the far West, Miss Kate, and shortly after you will start for my loved England's shore. I fondly trust that we may have the happiness of meeting again at some future day; still I would fain possess some little memento of these pleasant, and, to me, happiest hours of my life.

"Have you a photograh, or any likeness of yourself that you will give me as this memento?"

For a moment my poor heart stood still! Conflicting emotions rushed through my brain. Was he trying to feign an interest in me simply because he thought it to be his duty, while he felt it not? What did he want of *my* poor little phiz? For aught I knew he was then wearing the Lady Alice Irving's, encased in gold, and perchance surmounted by pearls.

My pride was roused! He should know that he could not deceive me, and that any feigned interest in me would be treated as it deserved. I replied, therefore, quite scornfully, "Do I hear Sir Henry Vernon aright? What does he wish of *my* photograph, and why does he wish a reminder of *me* in his absence?

"I know it is a very common thing, in these days, for the young ladies to have their photographs taken by dozens, and bestowed upon any one, from a beardless youth to a gray-whiskered man, for the asking! He must excuse me if I said that I never yet had bestowed my likeness on any man, and I never would, unless he was a near relative or personal friend!"

"Am *I* not a personal friend," asked Sir Henry, in a grieved tone of voice.

"Yes! but you are engaged to the Lady Alice Irving; and if I were engaged to a gentleman I should not wish him to have a host of other ladies in his possession, to be gazing at continually; so you see I do as I would be done by!" with a ghastly attempt at a smile.

Sir Henry looked at me a moment as though he would read my soul, and then replied, in a soft tone, "Miss Kate, do you really believe me to be engaged to the Lady Alice?"

"Certainly," replied I; "I learned it before I had the pleasure of an introduction."

"Then, Miss Kate, you will allow me to say that I was never engaged to her or any other lady!

"I trust you will excuse me, Miss Manton, if I have been guilty of impropriety in my request, for I felt and intended anything rather than disrespect!"

If such a thing could be in these days as a gentleman in tears, I should most certainly have believed that Sir Henry was going to weep. His lip quivered, and he turned away his head to conceal his emotion.

Never did I so hate myself as at this moment; and yet my heart leaped for joy that I had heard from his own lips that he was not engaged!

After a moment, I said, with some little hesitancy, 'Mr. Vernon, I am truly sorry if I have wounded your feelings, — I intended nothing of the kind.

" The fact is, the price of photographs has placed it so completely in the power of every one to have them taken in any number, to say nothing of the tintypes, which may be obtained for about a cent and a half apiece, that you find even children will have their pockets filled with the faces of all their uncles, aunts, cousins, and friends, of every size and age, which they carry around as though they were marbles.

" I was always sensitive on this point. The likeness of my friends are too sacred to me to be treated in this careless way.

" There are instances where young men, whose friendship would not be desirable, will have in their possession the likeness of some estimable girl, who would blush to be seen in his company, who will hand around this likeness as though she were an intimate friend, when he received it from some other person, who did not care for its possession !

" I trust you will not misunderstand me !

" I consider photographs one of the most desirable inventions of the age ; but I am very careful that none of mine, or my dearest friends, shall ever be in the possession of any one who will not value them."

"Am I not one of your true friends, Miss Kate?" said Sir Henry.

"Indeed you are," I replied; "I esteem you as one of my most valued personal friends; and, had I have taken a few moments for reflection, I should not have wounded you, nor myself through you.

"If you would really like my picture as a reminder of the pleasant days that we have passed together, I shall be only too happy to present one to you before you leave, but I shall certainly expect one of your own in return."

"Which you shall have, most certainly!" replied Sir Henry.

APRIL 14th.

Sir Henry has gone this morning, and I feel *so* homesick!

I cannot understand it.

Why is it I should have such strange feelings stealing over my senses as I had when I first went to boarding-school, and which the scholars call homesickness? Here I am in my own dear home, with pa, ma, and Frank; the sun is shining bright, and Arty, my pet canary,—Minnie named him,—

singing till he almost deafens me. Minnie is coming in to pass the afternoon, and next week I am to start for England; and yet, and yet, I don't care one straw for England, or any other place save the West!

If I could choose, I would give up the realizing of all the fond anticipations which have filled my heart for so long a time, of wandering about in the haunts of Burns and Scott, to say nothing of Bunhill Fields, where the loved and gifted Bunyan lies; and, the fondest of all, to gaze upon the grave of the " Dairyman's Daughter," could I only start off in the train that leaves for Chicago at eight o'clock this morning, and be with that *precious* lamb again!

What a fool you are making of yourself, Kate Manton!

I should be ashamed to avow such weakness! A lamb, indeed! I think Sir Henry would thank you for the compliment!

Sir Henry came last evening to bid me good-by. He stayed until the hand pointed to eleven. It seemed as if he could not leave!

He handed me his photograph, which I minutely

examined, and declared it needed only speech to make it real!

"You are the only lady who has ever received a likeness of me, Miss Kate; therefore I presume it will not be taking too great a liberty to ask the fulfilment of your part of the agreement!"

Of course I had to give him one of my, to say the least, uninteresting-looking faces, so I handed him three from which to select; and, if you can credit it, dear Diary, he said, " If I would not consider it *too* grasping, he would take the three, as each one had some merit in itself which the others did not possess!"

I replied, " I could not think of such a thing!" but he very gravely took out his pocket-book, and placing them in, said, " By your · permission I will select one during my trip out West, and, should you insist, on my return I will hand you two of the three." Of course I could not refuse him, he uttered it so gracefully!

And he has gone!

And *I* am alone. Never so much so as now.

But I have one sweet solace. The darling, precious little photograph which is never away from me. No one knows my secret but you, my Diary, and I know that you will never betray my tender soliloquies over it to the cold world!

I fear I shall not intrust much else to your keeping before I arrive in Europe. Still, there are one or two items of information which I have acquired this last week, and which, unless I give them to you now, I fear may slip from my memory.

The first is *Schiller*, the German poet, dramatist and historian. He was born in Wurtemburg, a hundred years ago and more, and was the author of the celebrated *drama*, "William Tell."

Rossini, also, a celebrated Italian musician, born eighty years ago, lately deceased, who composed the famous *opera* of "William Tell," "Gazza Ladra," "Semiramide," and a host of others, not forgetting the thrilling "Stabat Mater!"

Sir Henry also mentioned *Lady Mary Wortley Montague* one evening, at Mr. Maverick's, and I must remember something about her.

She was born in England a little more than a hundred years ago; and, as a lady of wit and fashion, was very prominent in her time, and her letters hold an eminent place in that species of literature.

She was the eldest daughter of the Duke of Kingston. When only eight years old, she passed what she termed the happiest day of her life, in the "Kit-Cat Club," consisting of some of the most eminent men in England, into which she had been elected in a frolic.

At twelve she wrote a poetical epistle from Julia to Ovid.

Ovid was a celebrated Roman poet, who was much in love with Julia, daughter of the Emperor Augustus, and who lived in the time of Christ.

At fifteen, Lady Mary meditated the establishment of a nunnery.

She was a great friend of Pope, who was the greatest English poet of his time, but who afterward became her greatest enemy, because she could not refrain from a fit of laughter, when, at an ill-chosen moment, he was making love to her.

There is the dinner-bell, so I must now find food for the body instead of the mind.

I thought, two hours since, I should taste no food to-day, I was so sick, — so *home*sick! How true it is, if we can only divert our mind instead of brooding on our sorrow, we shall very soon regain our former equanimity. It is certainly true in my case, for I feel as though I had been fasting for a week!

Half-past 10, P. M.

Minnie passed the afternoon with me, and intrusted me with a most joyful piece of news. She is going abroad with me!

Now the secret mystery hanging around ma and Minnie, — their whisperings, their many signs, — is disclosed.

Mr. Maverick had business in Liverpool which could be attended to by no one save himself. He would take charge of me to Liverpool, if grandpa would take charge of Minnie on his arrival there. Ma wrote grandpa, and the answer returned that " he should be very happy to be her protector, not only on his own account, but because it would so greatly enhance my happiness."

Mr. Maverick insisted on procuring my ticket, and presenting it to me. Ma was candid enough to inform him that grandpa had sent me a check for that purpose.

" Very good," he replied; " then she can retain that for spending-money ! "

Noble, disinterested man! How he loves to gladden the hearts of those who are less favored with this world's substance.

If I am not greatly mistaken, I shall spend two-thirds of it, at least, on my own loved ones at home.

Frank shall surely have a new suit for his examination at Harvard.

To-night is Thursday; and Tuesday next, Providence permitting, I shall start for my loved Sir Henry's native land. I blush to confide even to you, my Diary, what I wish; but if it is ever gratified, you shall know it !

XII.

W E arrived in Liverpool a week since, where we took the cars immediately for London. Mr. Maverick found a friend who was going down on that train, and intrusted us to his care.

On arriving at the depot in London, we met grandpa, who was overjoyed to see us. His carriage was in waiting, and we were taken to his mansion in Belgrave Square, which is in the part of the city called West End.

I had no idea of the size of London. I always conceived of it as a large place, but much after the similitude of New York! Any one who has visited it under the same impression, can judge of my complete surprise.

Grandpa informed us that London was from six miles and upwards in extent, and was properly divided into the Old City and the West End.

The city was mainly the business part of the place; at West End were the royal residences, mansions, gardens, and the like.

The day after our arrival, grandpa ordered the carriage for a drive.

We drove through Kensington Gardens, St. James' Park, and then through Regent's Park.

When I compared them with those of our own land, I could but be amused.

The bare idea of calling our few acres, with an iron fence around, — a few gravel walks, with a fountain here and there, — and an occasional iron chair or seat, some trees and spots of grass, a *park!*

And yet I own to a little chagrin; for there is no good reason why we should not have parks, not only to vie with, but to surpass even, old England!

Here in England, the parks are composed of hill and valley, river and pond, — gigantic trees of ancient date, long stretches of grass-plats, rare plants,

13

— good roads instead of walks, affording ample room for the many elegant equipages which are constantly passing through them.

Hyde Park is one of the famous drives of the Queen. Grandpa said that we should drive through there the next day, and that we should probably see the Queen, — at least, we should meet the Prince and Princess of Wales; but the next day proving rainy, our ride was deferred another day.

Grandpa was to attend the Queen's drawing-room on Friday, and insisted, at first, that Minnie and I should accompany him; but as we had neither of us provided ourselves with dresses suitable to appear in the presence of royalty, we thought best to decline.

As it was no new thing for grandpa to be present at these receptions, he also gave up going, and ordered the carriage, to take us a drive around the city in the evening, that we may see it by gaslight.

The old city is under the care of the Mayor, and contains but little more than a hundred thousand inhabitants.

We drove by Charing Cross, which grandpa says took its name from the old village of Charing, where Edward First erected a cross.

Charing Cross and Trafalgar Square are the great turning-points from the West End to the city. The cabs start from Charing Cross in so many different directions, that grandpa says it is often called " the centre of cabs."

In Trafalgar Square is a column erected to the memory of Lord Nelson, the great English admiral. There are statues, also, of George Fourth, Havelock, and Napier.

There is also a rider seated upon a horse, which is said to represent George the Third. At the gates of the Square are immense bronze lions! The square was illuminated with large globe-like lamps.

We drove through Pall Mall, and Regent Street. The streets were brilliant with gas-light. There were reflectors furnished with burners on the outside of many of the windows, to throw light on the goods displayed within.

Grandpa informed us that London numbered nearly, if not quite, eight thousand streets. He drew our attention to one spot, called the Seven

Dials, where seven streets branched in different directions, and which he reminded us was spoken of in Dickens's works. I did enjoy the evening drive!

The next day we drove out to see some of the lions of London.

Our first visit was to Westminster Abbey. This is the place where the British Sovereigns receive their crown. It is the great church of the West End. Its existence is traced back to the early part of the seventh century. It is in the form of an irregular cross. All of the British Sovereigns, from Edward the Confessor to Victoria, were crowned there, and many of them are buried beneath its sacred walls.

Surrounding the east end, in a semicircle, are nine chapels, the most interesting of which are those of Edward the Confessor, beyond the altar, and of Henry the Seventh, which forms the eastern extremity of the Abbey. The centre of the former chapel is occupied by the shrine of Edward the Confessor.

I asked grandpa why he was called the Confessor?

He said that he was canonized and styled Confessor

about a hundred years after his decease; and that he was also called " Good King Edward" by the people, who remembered him with affection, on account of his strict justice in the administration of his government. But he had many faults, one of which was that he imprisoned his mother for life in a monastery, because she tried to prevent him from obtaining the throne. Still he was noted for his sanctity, and his laws and customs were long remembered with popular affection.

The monuments of Queen Elizabeth and Mary Queen of Scots are in the north and south aisles of the chapel, respectively.

In another part of the church is a space called " The Poets' Corner," where are monuments to Dryden, Thompson, Shakespeare, Goldsmith; also to Macaulay, the historian, and Stephenson.

Religious service is performed daily in the Abbey, as also services on Sunday. We are to attend service held on Sunday forenoon, and at St. Paul's in the afternoon.

To me the famous Westminster seems more like one vast tomb, than a place of worship for the living.

Here was the dust of royalty; — kings and queens, who in years gone by had been the great ones of earth; and now where are they?

What more vain than human greatness, for which peace, love, yea, even life itself, is sometimes sacrificed!

Well may the preacher say, " Vanity of vanities, *all* is vanity!"

After passing an hour or more in this sacred place, we visited the British Museum.

My attention was directed chiefly to the examination of the wonderful curiosities which had been deposited there from Babylon and Nineveh. To think that these identical sculptures and bas-reliefs had been gazed upon, in ages long gone by, by Nebuchadnezzar and his subjects, by Eser-haddon and Sennacherib! I would sooner gaze on these mighty monuments of the truth of God's Word, than on all the palaces and works of art that London contains.

After gratifying our curiosity for another hour, we drove to St. Paul's.

This is the cathedral church of the See of London. It stands at the head of Ludgate Hill, on the site of the old St. Paul's, which was destroyed in the great fire of 1666. It is surrounded by a street which bears the name of St. Paul's Churchyard. This street has buildings on one side of it, and on the other is the iron palisade which forms the enclosure for the open yard or space on which St. Paul's stands. In the interior of the dome is the famous whispering-gallery, which connects with the stone gallery on the outside of the dome. The ascent is between six and seven hundred steps; but we were too much exhausted to attempt climbing them, although we learned that the dome was divided into compartments, which were covered with paintings that had the appearance of being very ancient, though they have been lately retouched by artists and painters employed for the purpose. I saw here monuments, also, to departed greatness, — one to Dr. Ben Jonson, and another to Nelson.

The great bell of the church is said to be ten feet in diameter. Grandpa says we will visit it again, when we are less fatigued, and devote more time to its examination.

On Friday we drove out in time to see the elegant procession of carriages, with their heraldic devices, filled with the lords and ladies who were to attend the Queen's drawing-room at St. James. Grandpa insisted that on our return from our proposed tour in France, and some of the other noted places in Europe, that we should be provided with suitable apparel, and attend the drawing-room with him.

He thought the expense would be as nothing, when compared with the honor of an introduction to the Queen.

I told Minnie, after we were alone, that I should rather by far appropriate the money for a different purpose.

She was very anxious to know what *could* afford me more pleasure than to visit the palace, and to see and speak with the Queen.

I told her that I wanted to visit the old kitchen, look upon the heraldic sculptures, and sit down in the wide old fireplace, in the Mansion-house at Stoke-Pogis! Then, too, I wanted to see the small room in the Manor-house, where are the rude paintings on the plastered walls, and the quaint inscriptions, " Feare the Lorde," " Beware of Mallis," " Beware of Pride," and others.

I should like to visit the old churchyard, and find,

if I can, the very spot where the touching Elegy was written, —

"The curfew tolls the knell of parting day."

Could I but choose my own friends and associates, I should select such as Gray, Cowper, and Scott; but the trouble is *they* would not select *me!* Poor, insignificant mortal that I am, never feeling my utter insignificance more deeply than when dwelling on the lives and gazing on all that remains of such gifted ones!

TUESDAY, 10 P. M.

My desire has been gratified. We have visited Stoke-Pogis, and seen the venerable church. It is from two to three miles from Windsor, far removed from the public highway, and within a fine old park, which grandpa says formerly belonged to the family of William Penn.

On a tablet under the east window of the church is the following inscription : —

"Opposite this stone, in the same tomb upon which he so feelingly recorded his grief at the loss of a beloved parent, are deposited the remains of

Thomas Gray, the author of the 'Elegy written in a Country Churchyard.' Buried August, 1771."

A plain, unpretending tomb covers the poet and his mother.

West End Cottage, his residence, has been much enlarged and beautified; but it was the same charming spot to me.

I cared not to see the spot where the Henrys, or the Williams, or the Georges rest, — but the country churchyard of Gray is precious and sacred to me.

We have visited, also, Bunhill Fields, and looked upon the spot where the immortal Bunyan sleeps; and then dear grandpa, who is beginning to discover what will afford me the greatest satisfaction, ordered the coachman to drive us to Bedford, where we visited the jail, and I sat down in the room where our loved Bunyan was kept a prisoner for twelve years. There I thought, as I sat alone, — for I persuaded grandpa and Minnie to leave me for awhile, and explore the rest of the jail, — of the wonderful book that he there penned, " Pilgrim's Progress," and how many souls had been led to heaven by it, — how many had been cheered by its quaint illustrations, and saved from falling into the power of Giant Despair! and then I wished that I could see the house where he was born; but it would really be imposing on good nature to ask grandpa to drive us there. As I meditated, the kind man made his appearance, and said, "Well, Kate, if you pass the day in the jail, we shall not have time to visit the old homestead."

How my heart leaped for joy! I could only say, "Grandpa, how could you know my heart so well?"

"Ah, Kate!" he replied, "who should know your heart if not your old fond grandpa?"

We rode about a mile, when we passed a large sign-post with *Elstow* on it, in unmistakable characters.

Elstow, the birthplace of Bunyan. A dear little village, just such an one as I should imagine the birthplace of such a man; and in a few moments we stopped at the gate and gazed upon the revered walls of the old homestead. There was a rustic rudeness and simplicity about it; and, although grandpa said it had been standing for upwards of two hundred years, yet it looked as if it may stand a century longer. A pleasant, mild-looking old lady opened the door, and asked us if we would

like to come in; but as the house had undergone
repairs and alterations, we thanked her, but thought
we had better postpone our visit inside till some
future time.

THURSDAY.

To-day we have visited the famous " Tower of
London." I was particularly interested in it as
being the prison of Sir Walter Raleigh for thirteen
years, six years of his imprisonment being shared
by his wife, and who, although he was released, was
never forgiven his supposed crimes, but was afterward beheaded.

We entered the room in which are kept the
crowns and sceptres of the Kings and Queens, as
also their diamonds and state jewels. These treasures are placed in a large iron cage, where one
can see, but not touch them.

Nothing, however, has touched my feelings so
much as the sight of the block and axe that were
used at the execution of Anne Boleyn and Lady
Jane Gray.

We saw the marks in the block that were made
by the blows from the axe.

Poor Lady Jane! Although the great-granddaughter of Henry the Seventh, and granddaughter of Mary, the young widow of Louis the Twelfth of France, she suffered, even in her earliest childhood, from the rigorous treatment of her parents.

She accepted the throne of England with great reluctance, yielding only to the wishes of her father, and husband, Lord Dudley. She reigned only for a few days, and then was confined in this Tower with her husband, and in a few short months, by the order of Queen Mary, they were both beheaded, —she in the Tower, on account of her royal blood, her husband on Tower Hill.

To-morrow we start for Paris; so I must lay by my pen, and repack my trunk.

MAY 6th.

We arrived in Boulogne yesterday morning, having time only for a glimpse of the town. It is surrounded by ramparts which have been transformed into beautiful promenades planted with trees, and affording a magnificent view that extends to the coast of England, which is distinctly visible in clear weather.

After a slight lunch, we took the cars from there

to Amiens, where we stayed and passed the night, as we wished to visit the Cathedral.

This Cathedral, which was built just before 1300, is 415 feet long, 182 broad, and the spire is 420 feet high.

Grandpa says the interior woodwork is considered a miracle of carpentry; the two pilasters, or piers, being the only support of the great expanse of arches, so that nothing interferes with the view below.

The exterior is sculptured to a great extent.

Amiens was the birthplace of Peter the Hermit.

Minnie whispered to me that I should ask grandpa who *he* was?

In answer to my inquiry, he replied that Peter led the first company of Crusaders against Palestine. Now I remembered all about the Crusade, but had not the faintest recollection of the poor hermit, so I asked to be a little more enlightened!

Grandpa replied that he knew but little regarding this man, save that when the Crusade was first started a number of men formed themselves into a large company, and chose Peter as their leader, on account of his great enthusiasm and zeal in the enterprise; but that after they had started, some of the company separated from the others, and placed themselves under the command of "Walter the Penniless," when they were dispersed in a quarrel with the Hungarians.

On the conquest of Jerusalem, Peter preached a sermon to the Crusaders from the Mount of Olives.

After this, he returned to Europe, and founded an abbey, where he passed the rest of his life.

It was at Amiens where the treaty of peace was signed between Great Britain and the French Republic, known as the "Treaty of Amiens."

And now we are safely lodged in Paris, — the gayest city in the world.

Minnie and I had always prided ourselves on being fine French scholars, — but we were just nowhere! For a time we felt that we might as well be among the Chinese; but grandpa, with his usual thought, engaged us a first-class dress-maker for a week, explained to her our trying position, which interested her in us very much, and as we were wanting only in the Parisian accent, and the volubility of expression so peculiar to the French, and which, until one becomes familiar with their

style, renders it so bewildering, we were very soon
in a fair way of passing ourselves for Parisians!

We have made some very pleasant acquaintances
to-day, — one gentleman, in particular, who reminded me so strongly of Sir Henry.

We had some most delightful music in the eve.
One of Chickering's superb grand pianos was in
constant requisition. How Minnie and I were be-
sieged! If we only would gratify Mr. B, or Miss C.
At length Minnie complied, and performed, to the
great admiration of the company, Chopin's Grand
Polonaise, in E Flat. "Something from Liszt! something of Liszt's, Miss Maverick!" and, with a deal
of animation, she played one of his favorite *Caprices*,
which was received with unbounded applause.

Liszt is one of, if not *the* great favorite of the
Parisians. They always speak of him with the
greatest enthusiasm.

Hungary may well be proud of being the birthplace of *Franz Liszt*, for probably no musician
has been more honored, flattered, or caressed by all
ranks of society, than during his triumphal career

from 1837 to 1847. After that time, he received an offer, from the Duke of Weimar, to assume the post of Conductor of the Court Concerts and Opera at Weimar, which he accepted.

It is to his exertions that Wagner is indebted, in a great measure, for the publicity which his operas now enjoy. Liszt stands at the head of what has been called the "prodigious" school, excelling in the production of difficult and novel effects. His fingering is firm, vigorous, and wonderfully flexible.

THURSDAY EVE.

Yesterday we visited the Hotel de Ville. The high buildings, toppling over crooked lanes that surrounded it when grandpa last visited Paris, were swept away, leaving it in a spacious, open place, on one side of which palatial military barracks have been erected, while miles of broad avenues communicate with other parts of the town; the elegant parks of Bois de Boulogne, and the Bois de Vincennes, the gardens, squares, and fountains, bear witness to the improvements urged on by the Emperor. The Hotel de Ville is the finest municipal edifice in Paris. It is the residence of the Prefect of the Seine. Its public offices occupy nearly two hundred rooms, besides containing several halls in which the meetings of different societies are held, and a magnificent suite of state apartments.

The original front, displaying the architecture which prevailed in Italy during the sixteenth century, has been increased by two main bodies, flanked with pavilions in keeping with the old portion, the whole being adorned with Corinthian columns, and niches filled by statues.

But I cared very little for the architecture or splendor of the mighty building, — my eyes were riveted on that historical room, with which all the revolutions in France had been in some way connected.

I saw, with my mind's eye, Louis XVI., when he spoke to the populace with the " cap of liberty " on his head ; — and also the noble Lafayette, — a name ever to be placed at the side of Washington in the hearts of all true Americans, — when he embraced Louis Philippe, and presented him to the people, in 1830. Not many years ago, thousands and thousands surrounded this building, within which the Provisional Government were holding their first session, —

that astounding session of sixty hours! Grandpa was in Paris at the time; and he says that while the flags were waving, drums beating, and shouts rending the air, the doors of the hotel flew open, and Louis Blanc stepped forth and announced "A Republic!"

We next turned our steps to the united palaces of the Louvre and the Tuilleries. Grandpa informed us that its width measured 1,008 feet, and that the distance from the eastern colonnade to the western front is half a mile; that its roofs cover, beside the Museum of Arts, a library of 80,000 volumes, and quarters for several regiments of troops; the offices and private apartments of the Minister of State, the private and state apartments of the Emperor and his household, the Imperial chapel and theatre, and palatial stables for Imperial horses!

Next we visited the museums of the Louvre, which are twelve in number.

They occupy the magnificent palace, completed by the labors of successive French monarchs, from Francis First to the great Napoleon.

We passed an hour or more examining the old paintings, also the Assyrian and Egyptian antiquities.

I have a great passion for the ancient and the marvellous!

I well remember, when a child, visiting a museum; and while the rest of the party were examining the different objects of interest, I stood, almost entranced, gazing in speechless wonder at two *mummies*, — and it was with difficulty I could be persuaded to leave them.

This morning we visited the Place du Carrousel. This is an immense palace court, whose principal ornament is a triumphal arch, designed after the arch of Septimius Severus of Rome.

It is adorned by eight Corinthian columns of red marble, with bronze bases and capitals, and surmounted by a triumphal car, with four bronze horses.

The west side of this court is enclosed by the main body of the palace of the Tuilleries, whose western front looks on the gardens of the same name, with their flowers, fountains, and orange-trees.

We next visited the Place de la Concorde. In the midst of this square, between two magnificent fountains, rises the obelisk of Luxor, a monolith seventy-two feet high, first set up in front of the great temple of Thebes, thirty-four centuries ago, by the great Sesostris, who was one of the early kings of Egypt. Grandpa informed us that he killed himself, so it is said, after a reign of sixty-six years, because he feared he was growing blind.

The waiter has just handed us each a letter, — Minnie's, of course, from Arthur. Who is the author of mine I cannot divine, for it is an unfamiliar hand.

I opened it, — what kept me from screaming or showing some symptoms of great trepidation, I cannot say; but as I turned over and looked at the signature, — Henry Stuart Vernon, — my head grew dizzy, and I thought I should faint; but, fortunately, I rallied before Minnie noticed me, and perused the epistle.

I think as the 'constant opening and closing a letter is sure to wear it out in time, and as I shall most certainly read this at least three times a day, I shall copy it into my Diary, and then, with the original in my hand, I can read the loved words, e'en though they are in my own handwriting, constantly reassuring myself, by gazing on the blessed envelope, directed by that darling hand.

Poor Minnie was so completely engrossed by her own letter from Arthur, she entirely forgot to ask about my letter, taking it for granted it was from pa, or ma! I was a little alarmed, at tea-time, when grandpa remarked, "All well at home, Kate?" I replied, "Yes, sir!" But my fears were groundless, as Minnie was engrossed in conversation with Mons. Guigon, and heard neither the question nor the response!

My Dear Miss Manton:

I trust you will excuse the liberty I have taken in addressing you without permission; but the knowledge that, when one is far away from loved ones at home, how welcome a letter, e'en though it may be penned by one almost a stranger, has led me to cast aside my scruples, and follow the teaching of the "golden rule" in the matter!

Arthur and I arrived safely in Lexington on Tuesday last, and, after passing a day in examining the place and its localities, we resolved, on our way to Nashville, to stop and visit the "Mammoth Cave" of Kentucky.

We started on Wednesday afternoon, and arrived

late the same night at Greensburg, where we stopped and passed the remainder of the night; and the next morn started, with our guides, and some other travellers, who were on the same expedition, and who proved very pleasant companions, for the Great Cave.

It is said to be the largest of the kind ever yet discovered in the known world. We approached it through a natural bower of trees, growing on either side of a romantic and beautiful dell; at its termination is the great portal to this nether world, and you descend into it down some winding stone steps; then, if you choose, you can penetrate *fourteen miles* into the heart of the earth.

No impure air exists in any part of the cave; on the contrary, the air is delightful and exhilarating, and highly recommended for diseases of the lungs.

There are a number of small houses built within, to accommodate consumptive persons, and numbers reside there continually, finding great benefit.

Stalactites, of gigantic size and fantastic form, are found here, though none so brilliant and beautiful as adorn many other caves.

This remarkable cave contains two hundred or

more avenues, nearly fifty domes, twenty-two pits and three rivers.   There are the Gothic Avenue, and Gothic Chapel, Fairy Grotto, and many others. Some of the avenues contain large and magnificent stalagmite columns, extending from the floor to the ceiling.

A river, navigable by boats, affords a novel means for exploring these subterranean recesses.   Few forms of life are found within this cave; but bats and rats are abundant, and there are several species of insects. Two varieties of fish only have been discovered, and, what is a little singular, one is the *eyeless* fish, and the other, though with eyes, is entirely blind!

This visit, my dear Miss Manton, has been a constant reminder of our visit to the Falls!   Arthur is constantly mourning the absence of his Minnie.

I have locked my feelings in my own heart, and have not yet committed myself as to whether I am lonely or not!   I will leave you to be the judge.

I have alleviated my bitter loneliness, by examining three photographs, and trying to discover if they bear a good desirable remembrance of a certain absent friend of mine, as I am allowed by that friend to retain only one of the three, and I desire to possess the one which claims the highest merit.

Arthur is intending to embark in the next steamer, and to meet Minnie in Venice.

If I thought it would enhance your happiness as greatly as it would my own, I should most assuredly make one of your party. At times I flatter myself that it would, and then I confess that I am again in doubt.

Need I say that I wish a better understanding in regard to our mutual position?

I love you, my dear Miss Manton, as I never thought it would be possible to love, — but I prefer to plead my cause in person. Now, if you will send me a telegram on the immediate reception of this, of one single word only, I will be governed entirely by that little word.

I shall see your loved parents before I leave New York, and inform them of my action in the case.

I need not assure you I shall tremblingly await the arrival of the telegram, to see whether the answer is charged with two or three letters!

With renewed assurance of the tenderest sympathy and affection, receive this from him, who would be evermore   Your own HENRY.

And it has gone! That dear little word with *three* letters! for why should I trifle with such a noble, generous heart as his? He will not think me in too great haste, or as glad to jump at the chance as some of the wise would say!

I am not a flirt, and never was one! If Sir Henry tells me his preference is for me, and asks for an expression of my feeling toward him, why should I keep him in suspense that I may deceive him, if possible, into the belief that I am not thus easily won?

I don't believe in such nonsense.

If he is partial to me, and I know it, why should I try to hide from him that his attentions are agreeable?

I believe the foolish practice of keeping a lover in suspense, and trying his finest feelings in every possible manner, is the cause of there being so many male flirts among us! There are times when man loves to retaliate, and who can blame him?

In nine cases out of ten, a well-principled, honest, upright, whole-souled man, will be drawn tenfold closer to the object of his affection, if he finds that she confides in him, and believes him incapable of trifling!

And thus I have trusted Sir Henry.

Should he wrong me, the wrong will sooner or later return into his own bosom. If he proves worthy of my confidence, I shall be well repaid for my faith in him!

How fortunate for me that the telegraph office was in the hotel, so that I could send my message myself, and no one be the wiser!

No one has any suspicion as to whom is the author of my letter.

There is real pleasure in keeping my secret locked up in my own heart.

It is laughable to think how the " lords of creation " insist upon it that women cannot keep a secret!

I confess, however, to a strong predilection for arraying myself on their side of the question; yet there are exceptions to every rule, and I consider *myself* an exception!

There are a class of women who delight in running from one to the other, telling not only the news that they glean concerning others, but also all that relates to themselves.

I am happy to say that this class, either from self-esteem, or love of approbation, are on the wane. It really seems to be the ambition of woman, at the present day, to keep her own counsel, and to delight in refusing to gratify the vain curiosity of the multitude.

Women can keep secrets!

Women *can* be Masons, e'en though they may not recognize the grip, and have never seen the skeleton !

Women can keep secrets, as many a wandering brother, aye, and husband even, can testify.

To-morrow we start for Aix-la-Chapelle, and from thence to Cologne.

Minnie has teased me, for the first time, as to the author of my letter, and really went so far as to ask grandpa if he had heard my letter from home.

Whether he surmises or not I cannot say, but the only answer he made was " he never asked to hear anything which I did not freely communicate ";

so I anticipate no further trouble. I am *sure* that Minnie does not dream that it is from Sir Henry.

MAY 12th.

We arrived in Aix-la-Chapelle last evening, and to-day we have viewed the city, visiting the Cathedral as the place of highest interest.

This is remarkable not only for its beauty, but for containing the tomb of Charlemagne, which is in the centre of the building, and bearing upon it the inscription, "CAROLO MAGNO." On the west end of the building is a tower where relics are kept, which are so sacred that they are exposed only to the public gaze once in seven years, and then from the gallery of the tower.

For four francs each, we were allowed a momentary gaze into the chest which contained these relics.

The bone of Charlemagne's arm is encased in a crystal framework, the plates of which are joined together by bands of gold; his skull, which vulgar hands have polished brown and glistening, is encased in a huge head of silver; his hunting-horn, made of an elephant's tooth, lies by the side of the head; the cross which he wore suspended from his neck; two admirable silver shrines, incrusted with gold and jewels, and the bas-relief in gold which adorned the marble arm-chair of the great Emperor.

This city was the birthplace and favorite residence of Charlemagne.

For a long time the German Emperors were crowned here, and many of their portraits, together with the marble chair of Charlemagne,. are yet to be seen. The Cupola once adorned with the celebrated granite pillars of the Empress Helena, which Leo Third consecrated, was surrounded by three hundred and sixty-five bishops, among whom were two, who, according to the legend, rose from their tombs to replace their absent brethren!

To-morrow we visit Cologne, and from there we shall proceed to Berlin.

How I wish that time would permit us to visit Manheim, the place of Schiller's youth; Worms, where Martin Luther, the hero of the Reformation, was consecrated; Bonn, the birthplace of the eminent Beethoven; Frankfort, where Goethe was born!

THURSDAY, 10 P. M.

We arrived in Cologne this morning. This lovely place is situated on the left bank of the famous Rhine, and is connected with the opposite shore by a bridge of boats, nearly fourteen hundred feet in length.

Grandpa informed us that it received its name from Agrippina, wife of the Emperor Claudius, and mother of Nero.

This is where the celebrated Cologne water is made; and I am told that they have thirty manufactories employed in this work.

Cologne is famous mostly for its monuments, the most remarkable of which are its churches.

St. Peter's, with its famous altar-piece, representing the crucifixion of St. Peter, by Rubens, who presented it to the church in which he was baptized; St. Ursula's, with the ashes of the eleven thousand virgins in its golden chamber; St. Panthaleons, with the tomb of Theophania, the Empress of Otho the Second; and the great Cathedral, which is considered one of the finest Gothic works in existence.

The heart of Maria de Medici is buried under a

slab in the pavement. She was the wife of Henry Fourth of France, and died in Cologne, in the same house where Rubens was born.

FRIDAY, 9 P. M.

We are passing the night in Hanover, and shall dine to-morrow at Magdeburg, the town in which was the celebrated Franciscan school, where Luther supported himself for a year by singing in the streets.

Hanover was the birthplace of Herschel!

MAY 16th.

We arrived in Berlin about six o'clock last evening. This place is surrounded by a nearly circular wall, of more than ten miles, with seventeen large gates, and two small ones.

The Brandeburg Gate is remarkable for its architectural beauty, and the statue of Victory, driving four horses, the whole of copper. Among the statues in the public squares and places, I was the most delighted with an equestrian statue of Frederick the Great.

The palaces are remarkable, — the royal palace containing over six hundred rooms and saloons.

The old museum is a gallery of pictures and antique vases; the new one, opposite the King's Palace, is one of the finest in the world, comprising the Egyptian museum, arrayed and enriched by the celebrated Lepsius; a gallery of pictures and statuary, and the celebrated frescoes of Kaulbach in the stairway.

The armory is undoubtedly the finest in Europe.

I received a letter from ma to-day. Among other news, she writes that pa has given up the house in Harlem, and taken one on West 139th Street, New York.

It appears that Mr. Vernon wrote pa the day after I sailed, informing him that he desired the services of a good lawyer, to substantiate some claims that he had found in Kentucky; and as he wished to place it in the hands of some one in whom he could place implicit confidence, he was anxious that pa should undertake the job!

As pa found it would be much more convenient for him to be in the city, he took a house there,

15

as soon as he had apprised Sir Henry of his willingness to attend to the business.

On Sir Henry's receiving pa's letter accepting his offer, he enclosed, in return, a check for a thousand dollars, as retaining fee!

With what a delicate, generous soul Sir Henry is possessed! As if pa would need, or ask a *retaining* fee, with his poor, scanty income!

If he is successful, it may be the means of placing him in the position to which he is entitled, — the head of the bar.

Pa may be a Judge yet, — Secretary of State, perhaps! Who knows?

Minnie continues to studiously avoid mentioning Sir Henry, — whether from the fact that Arthur has confided his own secret belief to her, and she wishes to prove worthy his confidence, or that she feels him to be so entirely out of my reach that she will not waste words in badinage, I know not!

MAY 21st.

We arrived in Vienna this evening, en route for Venice. We passed a few hours in Dresden, the

Florence of Germany, and a .day and night in Prague.

We met, at the latter place, Edward Hamilton, an elder brother of Harry's, who was travelling for his health.

He is tall, well formed and stylish-looking, and,. what is best, he is very highly cultivated!

He appeared very much pleased at the meeting, and exerted himself to be agreeable. He gallanted us around to see the lions of the place, and seemed never to weary of pointing out any object that was worthy of notice.

He tendered Minnie his warmest congratulations on her engagement with Arthur. The time had not arrived for *me* to receive congratulations.

I thought how great would be their astonishment, could they know even a tithe of my cherished secret.

Never did I find it harder to hold a tight rein on my unruly member; but I shall receive the reward of my patience yet!

In the evening Mr. Hamilton and grandpa had a short discussion on the " Woman's Rights " question! I think Mr. Hamilton inclines to the belief that women should have the right of ballot, — but grandpa, who is bitterly opposed to it, cornered him completely; and I really think, if they could be in company for a week or two, he would finally agree with grandpa.

For the first time I ventured to engage in the argument! I found that Mr. Hamilton agreed with me in maintaining that woman's sphere was emphatically, from her physical organization, designed to be unobtrusive and quiet.

"Yes!" said Mr. Hamilton, "this is very true; still, if woman was intellectually educated for public life, she would be intellectually fitted for it. You know, Miss Manton, that even Bonaparte feared the political influence of a Madame de Stael, as much as of any man in his realm."

"Certainly," I replied; "I do not argue the question of woman's superiority or inferiority of intellect, but simply my belief that woman has her sphere. The moment that she leaves the place which God designed and fitted her for, and places herself amid the confusion and distracting elements of political life, she sacrifices those gentle qualities that have ever been her charm and loveliness. Her

destiny has, by a holy law, been fixed; when rightly
educated, she is fitted for her sphere, and *when she
keeps in it*, she is happy in the fulfilment of her
duty."

"Oh!" said grandpa, "if the women of our land,
instead of wasting their time in arguing as to the
right of ballot, *which they never can obtain*, — if
these very women would institute a different kind
of reform, they would immortalize themselves.

"Could they prevail on the mothers of the present
age, who, with few exceptions, provided their means
allow, delegate the early influencing and educating
of their children to the daughters of the Erin Isle, —
if they could prevail upon them to undertake the
care and education of their children themselves, it
would be the next step, at least, to depositing their
own vote in the ballot-box.

"The mother's influence is felt by the lawgivers
and legislators of our land. It is she that moulds
them, that instils into them her own views and pref-
erences. The *mother's* influence over her children
is universally admitted. What a responsibility is
resting on our women! How much of the dissipation of the present age is laid at her door, for the

non-fulfilment of her duties! Will not some of the
more noble-minded come to the rescue, and institute
reform in this particular?

"I recollect," continued grandpa, "reading a short
paragraph from one of our Southern writers on this
subject, which I think worth remembering. After
comparing 'women's rights' to a '*mental ignis
fatuus*,' the writer says: 'Let woman keep her
head and heart clear from all that may cause her
to lose sight of her true destiny, and be content to
be the keystone in that beautiful temple of liberty,
designed and executed by those noble spirits who
risked all in its erection; *for to her is intrusted
the training of the heart and head of those who
are to guard this model fabric!*'"

Oh, that women would check that restless, fever-
ish excitement to be what they are not, and to
change what is, for an uncertain future that may
break up and destroy the whole fabric of our social
life! —

Vienna is divided into the old and new city; but,
contrary to the general rule in modern cities, the
old city is the more fashionable of the two.

Its streets are compared to a spider's web, radiating from a central point, near the cathedral of St. Stephen.

The streets are narrow, but the houses are lofty. The Emperor's palace is an ancient, vast, irregular structure.

We visited the imperial library, which contains nearly four hundred thousand volumes, and nearly three hundred thousand engravings, being one of the largest and finest collections in the world.

We visited the cabinet of minerals, where we saw an aerolite weighing seventy-one pounds, which fell to the earth in Croatia, in 1751.

The great cathedral is the finest specimen of Gothic architecture in the world.

Its bell, cast from cannons taken from the besieging Turks, weighs nineteen tons!

JUNE 1st.

We arrived safely in Venice last evening. On our way from Vienna we passed through Marburg. We had only time, while there, to refresh ourselves with a lunch.

How much I desired to visit the ancient castle of the landgrave of Hesse, where the famous religious conference took place between Luther and Zwinglii!

Minnie and I are feeling as free from fatigue as when we first started upon our tour.

Can it be the thought of happiness in store that buoys our spirits up?

"Here is a new arrival," said Minnie, who was just then looking out of the window; "and, as I live, here is Arthur!"

How my heart leaped to my throat! And then, as she made no farther comment, and I thought he was alone, I was seized with sudden faintness.

"Why, Kate, what *has* come over you?" asked Minnie.

"Nothing," I replied; "it may be fatigue." But at this moment the waiter tapped on the door, and informed Miss Manton that there was a gentleman wishing to see her in number fifteen. I glanced at Minnie; but her face was stolid, so far as evincing any suspicion as to whom it could be was concerned.

As I entered the room, Sir Henry, — for it was he, — came forth to meet me, and, before I could recover from my surprise, he clasped me to his heart!

"You must not, Sir Henry," said I, trembling so I could scarcely stand.

"And why not, my darling? Are you not my own sweet love?

"Did not the blessed little word *Yes*, that flashed across the mighty cable, place the rivet in that chain between our hearts that needed but that little word to render it indissoluble forever?

"Away with your cold, formal engagements. *True love* knows *no* form! If a form must be used, it is only to the exacting papa or to the punctilious mamma.

"No, my darling Kate, I knew your heart was mine, the first eve I met you at Mr. Maverick's. I read it the moment I asked you if I had seen you in the horse-car, and mine was yours in return.

"The first cause that drew you to me was your kindness to the poor woman; for, thought I, any lady, who in this age of selfishness and incivility is willing to rise in so kind and modest a manner to give her seat to another lady, and a poor one also, must have some innate goodness; and when you accepted my proffered seat, I read in your dear eyes that I was not mistaken; you had a soul, — and in that glance our souls had interchanged feelings which *must* ripen into closer intimacy.

"I was persuaded firmly, darling Kate, from that moment, that I had found my second self; and I was not mistaken! You were constantly in my mind. The face of each lady that I passed was scanned, with the hope of meeting you again. Judge of my complete surprise when I saw you in the barouche with the beautiful Miss Maverick!

"Yes! it was I, dear Kate, who urged Arthur to call upon Miss Maverick on that well-remembered evening, — trusting that if I did not meet you, I could at least discover your name and residence; and you may imagine my joy, dearest one, when I found the same sweet face there, that had so impressed me.

"Before I lead you to the altar, precious one, I want you should interchange views with me, on the duties of husbands and wives.

"This is justice to both. It will be a prevention against those little misunderstandings which are so much to be deplored in married life.

"If men and women would be more sensible in this respect, — if, instead of rushing headlong into an engagement and marriage, simply because they fancy a pretty face, a well-filled purse, or a stylish figure, knowing nothing of the disposition, character, or principles of each other, — they would associate together, with the understanding that if on closer acquaintance they find it will add to their happiness to be united in the bonds of matrimony, I think much misery might be prevented.

" But the custom of the day, and a foolish custom too, is, that when a gentleman has called upon or paid any little attention to a lady for a dozen times or less, every one that she meets must question her. as to whether she is engaged or not; and it requires a deal of moral courage for any lady to treat such shallow remarks with the contempt it deserves."

We remained for half an hour, enjoying this happy interchange of feeling, when grandpa entered the room.

I introduced him to Sir Henry, who informed him that he was betrothed to me with my parents' full and hearty consent; and asking for his benediction, which grandpa, as he had known Sir Henry by reputation for a long time, most cordially gave.

After a short conversation, Sir Henry took a card from his pocket, and writing on it a few lines, handed it to the waiter.

What he wrote I could not divine, but as it was no concern of mine, I gave it no farther heed.

In a few moments, however, the door opened, and Arthur, with Minnie, entered, and then the mystery was solved.

Such an excitement as existed for a few moments!

Minnie knew nothing whatever of Sir Henry's penchant for me! and confessed to thinking it was perfectly absurd for me to allow him to enter my mind, save as an every-day friend, and this was why she had been so silent regarding him!

"You shall have the medal, Kate, for keeping a secret," said Arthur.

After a pleasant chat, we separated to dress for dinner.

XIII.

SUCH a charming sail as we enjoyed this afternoon. Grandpa thought the young people would enjoy a row, and therefore he would take a nap.

Dear grandpa! I think he must have remembered his days of lovedom!

Minnie and Arthur engaged one gondola, while Sir Henry and I occupied another.

As we rowed along, the very beauty of the scenery seemed to inspire new emotions of love!

"I don't know of any more fitting place, my dear Kate, than the present, for me to give you my views on marriage. The truth is, I am in haste to open my heart to you, that I may be relieved from the suspense which I feel, lest you should decline becoming my precious wife! and yet I think it a duty which I owe both myself and you!"

How pale my darling looked when he uttered these words. I verily believe, had he have told me I was ever to do his will, without a why or a wherefore, I should have replied, " I know no will but thine ! "

Sir Henry commenced by saying that without this perfect confidence one towards the other ; without we were willing to undeceive each other, and own our peculiar habits, dispositions, tastes ; in a word, as ready to confess our faults as our virtues, he feared we should be obliged to adopt Lady Blessington's opinion : " Paying for a month of honey with a life of vinegar ! "

And, that there should be no deception between us, I must first know that he was of a *jealous* nature.

" I would not trust myself," said he, " to marry a woman that was a flirt.

" My wife must be mine own ; every look, every thought, must be mine ; therefore I could never submit to my wife's waltzing, — scarcely dancing, even, — with any partner but myself. Nor should I wish her to desire it even. You may call me weak, dear Kate, but it *is* my weakness ! Is your love for me strong enough to make me a promise like this?"

When I answered quickly in the affirmative, he replied, "Well, my dear one, I make you the same promise in return, though you may not own to the same demon!"

I answered that I should be quite as miserable to see him flying about with his arm around another, as he would be to see me in the same situation.

"Then, love, I am *exacting!* too much so altogether; but I am striving against it, and you must be patient with me.

"I am *uncharitable* towards the world at large, although my conscience is constantly reminding me. that the greatest virtue is *charity!*

"There are times when I am misanthropic, but with such a darling wife to gladden my home, I trust I shall rise above this foible. I am quick, impulsive, often saying the things I do not mean, and sowing for myself seeds of repentance.

"And then, Kate, my sweetest love, the greatest weakness, if you call it so, is yet to be told; my wife must pet me, — must love to sit upon my knee, and not crush down all tokens of earnest love as though they were childish!

"Say! can you be happy, my Kate, with such an one as I?"

"Happy? Oh! Mr. Vernon, you do not know that your faults are as nothing when compared with mine. My only wonder is, what *could* draw you to such a poor, weak, insignificant being as I am! Yes! weak, vain and frivolous! And yet, in justice to myself, not so much so as formerly.

"I am learning every day what it is to live, in the true sense of the word.

"I feel that I am responsible to God for all the talents which are intrusted to me; in fact, my afflictions have taught me that there is no happiness out of Christ. Though I am conscious of my own shortcomings, yet I feel that through Him I shall be strengthened to perform my duty.

"But no one knows my ignorance as do I myself. I know but little of the history of the world, either past or present, and I feel that I am not the highly-cultivated, well-informed person that such a man as you should call wife."

"I have no fears on that score, my darling Kate.

When we are settled in life, it will be a delight to study together. If it is agreeable to you, I shall pass the first year of our wedded life in travelling, not only through Europe, but also in Egypt and Palestine.

"I should like to pass two months in Greece alone, and learn of Homer and of Hesiod, of Sappho and Nicander, and of its mighty sons, Socrates, Demosthenes, and Plato! How I should delight, with you by my side, to stand on the summit of Mar's Hill, where Paul stood, and gaze around on the land where the mighty men of Athens lived and died!"

"It would be truly delightful," I replied; "but oh! Mr. Vernon, I feel myself so utterly unworthy such an one as you. I am so filled with faults of every kind!"

"And I feel myself no less unworthy, my sweet Kate; but my conviction is, that no marriage can be consummated with a fair prospect of happiness, save between those who make it a principle to disclose to each other their true characters. New scenes are sometimes unfriendly to harmony, and these develop new dispositions; but if there is no

intentional deception, they may be successfully en-
countered.

"And now, my dearest love, we will from this
moment, God helping us, be each other's world,
striving to promote in each other all those Christian
graces which will alone render us worthy of the
esteem and love of our fellow-man!"

"Mr. Vernon, you are the only man living that
I could love well enough to say, ' Your will is my
law.'"

"And Kate dear you are the only woman living,
to whom I am willing to intrust the keeping of my
future happiness.

"I feel that ours will be a happy union; and I
promise here, before God, to be to you a loving,
forbearing, indulgent husband!"

He then placed upon my finger the most exquisite
turquoise, surmounted by the richest pearls, saying
that he had departed from the custom of presenting
a diamond on the occasion, as this was his favorite
stone !

I assured him that if he had have consulted me
previously, he could not have more perfectly suited
my taste.

Venice is built on seventy-two little islands, into which piles have been driven; so that, from any point of view, the city seems to be floating on the water.

It is divided into parts, by the grand canal which runs through it in the form of an S, reversed. It is traversed by a large number of small canals, which run through the city in all directions.

They are crossed, so grandpa informed us, by three hundred and sixty bridges! Over the grand canal there is one only, — the Rialto.

It was from Venice that issued the first book published in Italy; and, in the seventeenth century, the first newspaper that was published in the world, which took its name from the coin called *gazzetta*, for which it was sold.

Our sail occupied so much of our time, that we visited only St. Mark's Cathedral. Grandpa says that Venice claims St. Mark as its patron and protector. More than a thousand years ago his bones were brought from Alexandria, and they then built this church in honor of him. On the top of the spire is the figure of an angel with outstretched wings. This is on the tower which contains the

bell, and is called the Campanile. It stands opposite the church, and to the top of the spire is four
hundred feet. The cathedral itself is built in the
form of a cross. There are five hundred marble
columns along its front, of various shapes and colors.
On its front entrance are four bronze horses. There
are also five domes to the church, the middle one
being the loftiest, and in each dome one elegant
picture done in Mosaic. The interior of the church
is marvellous. The pavement is of Mosaic marble,
and, as Sir Henry informed me, was designed to
represent the sea.

It certainly is one of the most magnificent edifices
that we have visited ; but in so short a time I could
not see half its beauties. I may visit it again, with
Sir Henry.

JUNE 6th.

We arrived last evening in Florence, which city
lies in a beautiful, well-wooded, well-cultivated valley, surrounded by the Apennines. We learned here
of the birth of a young Italian prince, who was
born at Genoa, and that there were great rejoicings
among the people. He is the son of the Duke

d'Acosta, — the second son of Victor Emanuel, — and has received the name of Emanuel Filibert, Duke of Apulia.

This afternoon we visited the beautiful villa, about two miles from Florence, which has been lately put at the disposal of the Grand Duchess Marie, sister of the Emperor of Russia, mother of Prince Eugene de Leuchtenberg, on account of his nuptials with Mademoiselle Apatchinine.

On the wedding-day the pilasters, doors, windows, and arches were festooned with the richest flowers. The chapel which we visited was gotten up in the Russian style. Byzantine pictures, rich crosses, painted glass, ritualistic candles, — in a word, everything that could set forth the peculiar rites of the Greek Church were there. Our attendant informed us that the bride, who in private received her mother's blessing, given with a sacred picture, had the picture borne before her as she entered the church and passed to the altar. The bride and bridegroom then partook of bread and wine, as emblematical of their united life.

Three times they were led around the pulpit by the priest, who covered their hands with the skirt of his garment, and chanted a prayer as he slowly performed this part of the ceremony.

Just in front of the pulpit was a small square of rose-colored satin.

I asked Sir Henry the meaning of this, when he informed me that it was a custom with the Greeks, and that it was considered emblematical of the lot of the newly-married couple; and also that the first foot that trod upon it *accidentally* (?) was the head of the newly-formed household!

A series of dinners and other entertainments are being given in honor of the nuptials. Sir Henry said that if we had the least inclination to be present, he had only to make himself known, and we should receive an invitation at once. But Minnie and I were so happy in the society of our loved ones, that we cared not for the pomp or vanity of this earthly grandeur.

Sir Henry whispered me that when I was his own I should be obliged to be present at all sorts of receptions, — balls, parties, and such like, — and therefore we would dispense with them as long as we could with propriety.

I suppose some of the young ladies would consider me *very* weak, and evince much surprise at my taste; but I had far rather know that I should be settled in some lovely spot, with a few true friends about me, than to feel that there will be comparatively few hours that I can call mine own.

But I will not dwell on those features of my anticipated married life which I contemplate only with weariness and disgust. I have been satiated with high life and its attendants in by-gone days; whether I shall enjoy it more when on familiar terms with nobility, remains to be proved.

I cannot, however, think them very unlike.

To-morrow we visit Pisa and Naples; but my most intense desire is to explore Herculaneum. I confided this desire to Sir Henry a week since, — it may be that he will remember it; if so, my desire will most surely be gratified.

This evening, while Sir Henry and I were promenading by moonlight, he said I may think him rash, but he was very anxious that, on our return to England, we should be wed at Helm Lodge!

He would telegraph to pa and ma, uncle Francis and brother Frank, to come over in the next steamer.

He informed me that his mother had a strange idea, when she was living; and that was, to buy and present the wedding-dress to his intended wife.

"Now, Kate darling, I will tell you why you heard it reported that I was to marry the Lady Alice Irving! I tell you, dearest, that you may feel perfectly at ease when you meet her! It was my mother's earnest wish. She is handsome, wealthy, and high-bred, — but such an one as I could not love. My mother was so constantly and publicly urging it upon me, that it really became a matter of notoriety.

"I think the Lady Alice was not aware that I had so deep an aversion to her. She fancies that I am obstinate, self-willed, and determined to have my own way, — that for some reason I did not fancy her, and, of course, shew her no particular attention. I always treated her deferentially, and shall continue thus to do. You may feel perfectly free when you meet her; and show, dearest, as little embarrassment as possible, as you will doubtless be subjected to her criticism and general surveillance.

" But I have no fears for you, sweetest; you will pass this or any other ordeal.

" My mother, however, trying to believe that I should eventually wed the fair Alice, purchased the wedding-suit, with diamond ornaments; a suit for the first reception, of an elegant rose-color of the faintest hue, and pearl accompaniments; and a pale blue brocade, with Florentine mosaics for the second reception! This was to suit her own fancy. She knew the Lady Alice was possessed of unbounded wealth, still *she* must wear them, or whoever the wife may be, out of regard to her.

" I will not deceive you, Kate dearest, by saying she would have purchased them for any other than one of the nobility, — for had she have imagined for a moment that I should have married an American, she would have disowned me! But she is gone, — the dresses are waiting for you to wear them, — and *how* happy shall I be when I see you arrayed in them ! " ,

How strange ! how inexplicable are the ways of Providence !

It had been one of my chief causes of anxiety how I should procure a wedding outfit, and here were

three of the most expensive garments already purchased, and waiting for me.

"Another thing, my Kate," said Sir Henry;
"you will have no necessity to provide anything for
our house, in the shape of housekeeping articles; for
as I was my mother's only heir, I inherited all such
articles with the house, and assure you that there
are chests stored away that contain of such articles
enough to last one a lifetime."

Here was another kind Providence! I couldn't
speak, — my heart was full to overflowing. Such a
delicate way as Sir Henry had of placing my poor
troubled heart at rest!

"But Sir Henry," I replied, "I cannot be married
at present; I must go back to my loved America, and
remain with my kind parents a short time; and
then, — please don't be offended, — I could not be
married by any one save my own dear Mr. Beecher!"

"Perhaps, Kate dear, Mr. Beecher might be persuaded to visit England, and perform the ceremony
at Helm Lodge."

"Well, my dear, kind Mr. Vernon, will you not
give me a little time to think of the matter before
I give you a decisive answer?"

"Certainly, Kate my darling; but remember that I am a lone man, and greatly in need of my wife!"

"Could you not go over to America with us, and pass a month, and then bring me back?" I inquired.

"Perhaps so, dear, if it will add anything to your happiness."

Sir Henry then handed me a note from my precious ma, which he said she told him to give me whenever the time for it arrived!

I did not ask what it was, for I knew by intuition that I should be required to gratify him!

JUNE 10th.

We are passing Sunday in Milan, where we arrived late yesterday afternoon.

This is a most charming spot, "standing as it were on green trees, as Venice stands on green waters," according to Raumer!

The principal entrance to the city is through the gate Tenaglia, by an esplanade called Piazza di Castello, containing an ancient Gothic castle of the Visconte family.

There is a street running all around the outside
of the city, called Strada di Circonvallazione. The
streets are well paved, but many of them are narrow
and winding.

There are not as many sumptuous mansions as
in Florence; but some of them are fine architectural
monuments, executed by distinguished artists, and
containing many works of art.

The cathedral of Milan, next to St. Peter's, is the
largest in Italy. It is one of the most wonderful
marble structures in the world, not only for its size,
but for its dazzling brilliancy when illuminated by
the sun, which gives it the appearance of having
been built of Carrara marble; but it is only the four
thousand statues which stand on brackets, or crown
the pinnacles, which are of this stone.

The building itself is of white marble, the pave-
ments being mosaic, in red, blue, and white marble.

The interior is crowded with monuments of
princes and prelates, and relics of saints.

The Amphitheatre of Milan, which was built in
Napoleon's time, would contain thirty thousand spectators, and is a favorite place for races, fireworks,

and balloon ascensions. The arena can be filled with water, and used for boat-races.

I remarked to Sir Henry that I could obtain a slight idea of the Coliseum in America, which was being builded in Boston for the Peace Jubilee, by looking at this building. I cannot understand what our New Yorkers were thinking about, to allow Boston to take the lead in such a matter. For my own part, I should have named *Washington* at once, as the only fitting place for such a great affair.

Ma writes that a great deal of fun is made about it, and that New Yorkers generally scoff at the idea of the Bostonians being able to accomplish anything; but we shall see what we shall see!

I myself am inclined to think it will be a success, for the Yankees always contrive, by fair means or foul, to accomplish all that they undertake!

The Coliseum in Boston is to be a third larger than this vast amphitheatre!

Sir Henry informed me to-day that my wish was to be gratified. I am to visit Herculaneum and Pompeii, and to take a bird's-eye view of Rome. He says we ought to remain a month in Rome to begin to see all the wonderful things there are to

be seen. Minnie and Arthur have a great desire to
see the Pope! but I think there are objects of far
greater interest that will attract me. Still, if time
admits, and there is a good opportunity to see his
reverence, I shall not object.

JUNE 14th.

I am writing in Rome, the home of the Cæsars,
made glorious by the birth of Julius Cæsar, whom,
having no equal in history as a General save Napoleon, — the highest rank as statesman, — as an
orator compared to Cicero, — as a writer only less
than Tacitus, — Shakespeare calls —

"The foremost man of all this world."

We visited first the Lateran church and palace.
This was founded by Constantine, and is the Epis-
copal Cathedral of the Pope, bearing over its chief
portal the inscription, "OMNIUM URBIS ET ORBIS
ECCLESIARUM MATER ET CAPUT"; which signifies,
"Mother and head of all the churches of the world!"
At its chief altar none but the Pope can read
mass, for it covers another ancient altar at which
the apostle Peter is said to have officiated. In front

of the church and palace stands a tall Egyptian obelisk, more than a hundred feet high, its red gray sides covered with hieroglyphics.

Grandpa informed us that it was broken, at one time, into three pieces, and was buried under the earth for centuries; then it was exhumed, and placed on the summit of the Cœlian, where it had stood for three hundred years or more.

We entered the church, and found it hung in drapery of red. Sir Henry informed me that it was the custom to vary the drapery with a color corresponding to the churches year. Red was the color of rejoicing, and decorated the church on and after Easter.

The ceiling was heavily panelled, and shone with gilding. The church is filled with monuments and pictures, as indeed are nearly all the European churches.

The Lateran palace was the home of the Pope, until he exchanged it for the Vatican.

Most of the monuments of ancient Rome have disappeared.

Nothing remains of the Palace of the Cæsars, which crowned the Palatine, but crumbling, beautiful arches.

The mighty Coliseum, which stands a little to the right, is not more than one-third its former size.

This immense amphitheatre was commenced by Vespasian, and finished by Titus; and when it was dedicated, there were from five to nine thousand beasts destroyed.

I had often heard of this immense building in my childhood's days, but I had no conception of its marvellous greatness.

Sir Henry said "that when it was first built it would accommodate eighty-seven thousand spectators, and that the arena was large enough for the combat of several hundred animals at a time."

It was founded on eighty arches, and rose to the height of one hundred and forty feet.

There were nets, made of wire, placed in front of the seats, to protect the spectators from the wild beasts. The seats were built of marble, but they were cushioned. The building itself was of travertine, faced with marble, while the arena was covered with sand. Every precaution was taken for the protection of the spectators, as its entrances were almost without number.

Subterranean pipes convey water into the arena, as at the amphitheatre in Milan.

We had a fine view, to-day, of Pope Pius the Ninth. We visited the Vatican, the residence of his reverence. Grandpa and Sir Henry are so well known, that we have only to express a desire, and we can be admitted to almost any place. The Pope was just going out for a drive, and, as he passed us, he gave a very condescending ·bow. He is a fine, open-faced, benevolent-looking old gentleman. One would hardly think him to have been seventy-seven years old last May; and yet those who have known him intimately say that he has grown older within the last five years, since he has had so many political troubles to contend with. He has much to fear, and he is aware of it, at the present day. He has found, to his sorrow, that it will not do to "put his trust in princes"! He is very liberal in his sentiments; so much so, that many of the Romanists have expressed great dissatisfaction at his many concessions.

The Vatican, the present residence of the Pope, is one of the most interesting and magnificent palaces in the world. It is in the north-western part of the city, about half a mile from the castle of St. Angelo, with which it communicates by a covered gallery!

The palace appears to be more á collection of 'separate buildings than one large edifice. Some idea of its size can be obtained by knowing that it has two hundred staircases or thereabouts, over *four thousand* rooms, and twenty courts! We entered the Sistine Chapel, and viewed " The Last Judgment," a magnificent painting of Michael Angelo's, and from thence into the Pauline Chapel, and examined the same mighty painter's frescoes of the Conversion of St. Paul, and the Crucifixion of St. Peter.

We next went into the museum connected with the palace. I must own that I am more dissatisfied than before entering it! So many wonderful , things to see, and so short a time to see them in, that everything was forgotten almost as soon as passed.

There were the vast number of inscriptions, three thousand or more, from ancient sepulchres and monuments; the sarcophagi of Helena and Constantia,— the mother and sister of Constantine; the picture-gallery, containing works of Raphael, Titian, Correggio, Guido, Veronese, and other painters of renown.

᠄ Great preparations are making here for the Œcumenical Council, which is to meet here next December.

It is said to be the first Council of the kind which has been holden since the time of the Reformation by Luther.

One should take a year to travel in Europe, and pass as much time in each place as will satisfy their desires. It seems to me like sitting down to a table filled with every sort of luxury, and eating your fill for one hour, and then leaving it, to taste nothing for a week. My only consolation is that Sir Henry has expressed the desire that we travel for a year after our marriage. The thought of living with the darling, as my own dear husband, is more than enough, though I may not see the outside of our house even for one year; but when I think of the additional happiness of travelling through this great land, I find the thought is almost insupportable!

JUNE 19th.

To-day I have consummated my ardent desire by visiting Herculaneum!

We arrived yesterday at the lovely city of Naples; but my whole thoughts were centred on Herculaneum. Herculaneum and Pompeii! What a magic spell clusters around these exhumed cities in my younger days. Let pa but say, " Here is some more news relating to discoveries in Herculaneum," and my attention was riveted at once. And even now I must confess to the same feelings of wonder and awe, connected with them when a child!

The morning was glorious; all nature was exuberant, — its whole face wreathed in smiles. The bees were banqueting among the flowers, — the hills in the distance rising far and blue, range above range, with the silvery clouds floating above them; gentle hills and valleys before us, — Vesuvius rising in the distance.

After a ride of about five miles, we halted at the ruined city. My wonder and curiosity were succeeded by such an indefinable sensation of fright, that had not Sir Henry been with me, with his reassuring smile, I should then have turned away, and dared not explore its subterranean recesses.

But I am *so* glad that I conquered my fears. One must visit the place himself, to form any idea of it.

That *theatre*, with its highly-ornamented walls, its floors and pillars of different-colored marbles, — the seats for accommodating its spectators, — when I sat down there and gazed, and thought how many hundred years ago those very seats were occupied by a people as careless and thoughtless as those who frequent the theatres in our own land, and that they should be buried while sitting there so instantaneously, so surely, with no way to escape their terrible doom, — it seemed too awful to dwell upon.

Then we passed, in the deep sepulchral gloom, along the streets, which were paved with lava, as in Naples. I found that most of the valuable relics, however, had been deposited in the different museums. We entered into many of the houses, and saw the cracked walls, which were propped to keep them from falling. The colors on the frescoed walls were fresh and uninjured.

Sir Henry informed me that there had been taken

from the ruins, statues, busts, candelabras, instruments of various kinds, musical as well as surgical, mirrors, cooking utensils, and paintings. Even the eatables themselves could be recognized in their charred remains.

They have also discovered some manuscripts, which are of no great importance.

Time forbade our visiting Pompeii; this pleasure, I trust, I have in reserve!

JUNE 23d.

We arrived in Genoa last evening, and took rooms at the Hotel Royal.

Grandpa can scarcely believe it to be the same place that he visited some years ago, with Irving.

He says that then it was called "*La Superba*," but he does not think it deserving the appellation now.

The reason he assigns for the change is, that the elegant palaces fronting the city, the homes of the nobility, are now transformed into hotels!

These palaces were frescoed externally when first built; but as that was many years ago, they look, now, anything rather than handsome,

This afternoon we visited the Palazza Rosso. Here was a fine collection of paintings, by some of the old masters.

Two of them particularly attracted our notice, — the full-length likeness of a young gentleman and lady. Our guide informed us that they were painted by Vandyke.

If I speak my honest sentiments, I must say I didn't think much of the churches in Genoa, either in style or architecture. One only is worthy of mention, — L'Annunciata, which was exquisite in its inside adornings, but rough and unfinished on the outside.

I felt more interested in Genoa, as it was the home of Columbus! We tried to find some mementos of him, but could find nothing but a monument, which was near the railroad station. It is really handsome, presenting a statue of the great navigator, with the different events in his life represented in bas-relief.

Sir Henry has just received a telegram announcing the death of his uncle, Sir Albert Fortescue Vernon, Earl of Somerset!

Sir Henry sent for me immediately on its recep

tion, and said that although the hour was late, he must talk with me awhile, as news of the death of his uncle had come upon him so suddenly, it had disconcerted all his plans.

He informed me that he was his uncle's sole heir, and that he had not only inherited his vast estate, but also his name and title, — he was no longer Sir Henry Stuart Vernon, but was now Albert Fortescue Vernon, Earl of Somerset.

"And now," to use his own dear words, "his hopes of making me his precious wife in old England were dashed to the ground.

"E'en though his people had have been apprised of the fact, propriety would not now admit it!

"But," he continued, "my precious Kate, although my disappointment is a bitter one, still I will not repine, but thank God that your precious heart is mine, and that with His blessing, before many weeks shall elapse, you will be my own dear wife.

"It will necessarily require all my attention to be concentrated on the settlement of this immense estate, according to English law, and it will take from three to six months before it can possibly be settled; and now, my darling, I need not assure you, that the moment I can leave conscientiously, I shall fly across the mighty deep, to claim my own love; and tell me, sweetest, will you be prepared to go with me at the shortest notice?

"One thought," said Sir Albert, — for he says I must call him so at once, that I may become used to it, — "extracts the sting from this disappointment; and this is, you will be able to fulfil your own desire to be for a short time in the bosom of your loved family."

Sir Albert is to leave at early dawn to-morrow; and at twelve o'clock, grandpa, Arthur, Minnie, and I, leave for Paris, and shall return from there to America immediately.

JULY 16th.

Once more I am sitting in my own dear home!

Can it be that in a few short months I am to leave it forever? I cannot bear to think of it; and yet I have a presentiment that I shall not long leave my darling pa, ma, and brother behind.

Something tells me that Frank will go to Oxford, rather than Harvard.

Dear old Harvard! I wish I could transplant

that with us. But I will not be so selfish. I seem
to be like some people I have heard of, — " the more
I have, the more I want." If pa and ma would settle in England with me, my happiness would be
complete.

I shall find no more time, at present, for writing.
Seamstresses and dressmakers, sewing-machines and
milliners, must now be in requisition; and yet I feel
as calm as if I was to marry an ordinary gentleman,
rather than one of the English nobility!

If I know my own heart, however, I would wed
Sir Albert, though I knew that I should have to
live on as scanty a salary as my father's!

But the main question seems to be, How I shall
raise the funds to furnish my wardrobe? Every
article must be of the finest, most expensive kind.

I have about three hundred dollars, — and this is
all! I suppose grandpa will remember me handsomely. I will do the best I can, and make the
money go as far as it will.

And it is all I *can* do.

Minnie has just been in, quizzing me a little.
" As if Sir Henry Vernon would think of such a
thing as looking at me, a poor drawing-teacher,

with six pupils, and my father the Clerk of the
House"! How Minnie laughed; and I laughed
with her! I could afford to!

JULY 26th.

Father has received a letter containing a check
from Sir Albert for two thousand, on account of the
law business. I keep my own counsel, but I verily
believe it is his delicate way of providing me with
funds. My package contained a blessed letter of
some fourteen pages; an exquisite miniature of himself, surmounted with gold and pearls, — one that
formerly belonged to his mother, — and also the
wedding-dresses his poor dear mother was so eccen-
tric in buying.

Do I believe in premonition?

It would be difficult to answer; but it certainly
was a little singular that this should have occurred
in my case!

The Lady Alice Irving would probably have
sneered at what is to me a very great blessing.

JULY 30th.

Oh, how the money flies! Fifty dollars is but
a mite in the balance.

How are all my wants to be supplied?

Fanny Hamilton has just called, and casually remarked that it was becoming quite fashionable to
write books in the form of a diary!

I wonder if I could bring myself to part with my
dear Diary for such miserable pelf as money?

And yet, money I *must* have!

Money I cannot do without!

Yes, I'll try it.

But what shall be its title?   Shall it be the one
that suggested itself when I first thought of writing
a book, — *Man's Wrongs ?*

It may not be amiss; for the day that heralds with
joyous shouts the advent of " *Woman's Rights*," shall
no less surely proclaim, with heart-rending groans,
the commencement of

" *Man's Wrongs !*"

August 6th.

Minnie called this morning, and brought me an
elegant set of Florentine mosaics, for a bridal gift.

I confided to her my pecuniary difficulties, — for
I can show my heart as safely to Minnie as to an
own sister, — and my plan for overcoming them.

" Why, Kate," said Minnie, " if you send your

manuscript to a publisher, you will not learn of its fate till you have been married six months!"

"I supposed it would be examined, and I should hear of its acceptance or rejection in a week, certainly," I replied.

"Why, no indeed," said Minnie. "I have heard of manuscripts being in the hands of the publisher for a month, without his acquainting himself even with the title! Sometimes they will pass from one publisher to another, till they are so soiled and dilapidated that the poor author is obliged to rewrite it, and considers himself fortunate if he disposes of it at all. I know for a fact of one publishing house who accepted a manuscript, and paid one hundred dollars down on it, and at the end of six years it was still a manuscript!

"An Alcott, Phelps, Stowe or Hamilton may not experience such treatment; but the great mass of writers have need of a large portion of the patience of Job.

"If the publisher has no place for a new book, he should say so at once, and relieve the author from the suspense in which he must remain until he learns the fate of his writings. I should be delighted for you to dispose of your Diary, Kate; but, even if accepted, it would not be published until it was too late for you to derive any benefit from it."

Just as Minnie uttered these words, Chloe called me, and said "two little girls wished to speak with me at the door." On obeying the summons, I found two of my drawing-scholars.

One of them, Carrie Knox, handed me a parcel, and asked me to accept it, with her love; the other, Sue Morris, gave me the tiniest package, and said it was a token of remembrance from her. On opening it, I found the loveliest gold thimble I ever saw, with my name engraved upon it. When I unfolded the package, words could not express my delight and gratitude to Carrie and her kind father. Carrie's father is the proprietor of a large dry-goods store on Broadway. My gift was half a dozen pieces of the richest lace, and French embroidery, edging and insertion. Minnie shared my pleasure, and assured me "that the way would be opened for me, if I could only retain my confidence and trust in God."

AUGUST 10th.

Grandpa came in to-day, and informed me that it was his wish my wardrobe should be suitable for the wife of so wealthy a nobleman as Sir Albert, and therefore I was to draw on him for any amount that was necessary to defray the expense. And now my heart is at rest!

Yesterday I received an elegant camel's-hair shawl from Mr. and Mrs. Maverick, valued at a thousand dollars; also a superb gold card-case, elaborately carved, from Laura Jenkins. It is surprising how generous my friends are in their gifts, when they know I am a *poor* girl!

I learned to-day that my much-admired Mr. Beecher had espoused the cause of " Woman's Rights." How depressing the thought! I can but hope it is a false report; for I cannot think so great and good a man would unite himself with such a misguided party!

I have also received a letter from Sir Albert, informing me that he cannot leave England until next spring, and that I must therefore make my arrangements to go to him, and be married at Helm Lodge, early in November. He will charter a steamer to convey the wedding-guests, and not one of my friends must be slighted. Grandpa, uncle Francis, pa, and ma, have held a consultation on the matter, and have concluded to gratify him.

Mr. Jenkins sent me, yesterday, a dozen gold spoons; and Belle brought me an elegant pearl cross.

I have been talking with brother Frank, and have offered him my Diary, telling him, if he can dispose of it, he may retain all he receives for it, as a parting gift from me. He thinks there is too little regarding the wrongs and rights of men and women, to make it acceptable. But I assured him that the subject was treated in *homœopathic* doses, and would produce a much more salutary effect!

If women will only receive the few hints which 'have been given them; rise from the degenerate state into which they have fallen, and try to imitate the character of the woman described in the last chapter of Proverbs, then shall we be, indeed, not only the *greatest*, but the *holiest* and *happiest*, nation on the globe.

www.ingramcontent.com/pod-product-compliance
Lightning Source LLC
Chambersburg PA
CBHW020343030726
47496CB00007B/1977